A Distant Beacon

Simon Quellen Field

A Distant Beacon

Illustrations and cover art by Simon Quellen Field

Published by MicroScience Press

19395 Montevina Road

Los Gatos, California, 95033

www.scitoys.com

First edition: December 2012

Second edition: February 2023

To Diane

Chapter One

Sarah woke in unfamiliar surroundings.

Not again.

Light was coming through a curtained window that should have been on the other side of the room. The curtains were the wrong color. The bed was too soft. And her head hurt.

She closed her eyes and controlled her breathing, trying to listen for any sound, holding back the panic. *Breathe in, then out, slowly, deeply, listen.*

There was a quiet fan somewhere at the head of the bed. There was movement occasionally outside the heavy door, but no sounds she could identify. The room was cold, and the light blanket was not nearly warm enough. There was a slightly unpleasant, but familiar odor in the room, like a disinfectant. She opened her eyes again, breathing slowly. She was in a hospital bed.

She felt the intravenous drip tubing taped to her arm, and considered removing it, but waited. There was a pulse monitor on the finger of her left hand. Removing that would bring a nurse, and she needed to be prepared before she attracted any attention.

She looked over at the window. From the light, it must be midday. She was in a private room. She began to lift herself up, to open the curtain, but the headache that had awakened her stabbed at the back of her eyes and blinded her. She lay back down. The stabbing became an oppressive throb, and she worked to control her breathing again. She worried that the pulse monitor was attracting attention, and she tried to slow her heart. She relaxed, trying to sink into the soft bed until it swallowed her up.

How long has it been, this time? She tried to remember the day before. Failing that, she tried to remember the last time she had eaten, or the last time she had left the house. No easy memories came. *It must have been a long one.*

She slowly raised a hand to her head, to massage the pain there. She felt bandages. And wires. There were wires attached to her head, under a layer of gauze and tape. A lot of wires.

What the hell?

Her mouth was dry, like she had been sleeping with it open all night. She wanted a drink, and to brush her teeth. *And a fucking aspirin.*

She remembered other times she had awakened in strange places. The first few were terrifying. Later ones were merely embarrassing and inconvenient, waking next to a man who called her by the wrong name, putting on unfamiliar clothes that fit perfectly, seeing herself in the mirror with the wrong haircut, or the wrong color. She had always managed to escape and get home, usually by playing along until she was alone and could slip away quietly. Never in a hospital.

She felt the bandages on her head, trying to follow the wires to the machine with the quiet fan. *This is not good.*

If it was a short one, she could usually remember things like her last meal, or the last time she had been out with friends. Nothing came to her this time. She pictured her house, imagined herself waking up, showering, picking out clothes, and then leaving the house to go — where? Nothing came.

She remembered her address. Her phone number. She waited tables at — *shit, where do I work?* She waited tables. In a sensible outfit, not some deep-cut cocktail waitress thing. A nice job at a

A Distant Beacon

nice place, not far from home. She'd find it. That would trigger the memories, and she'd be OK again. *We've been through this before.*

At least with head trauma they'd expect her to be a little dazed. That might make it easier to pass for normal, and to sneak out and back to her life. Or it might make it harder, they might want to keep her here, ask a lot of questions, getting the wrong answers. But she had to get out of here. Something deep inside was telling her something really bad had happened. *What did I do?* She decided she really didn't want to know. She just wanted to get away.

She'd need clothes. The flimsy hospital gown would keep her a prisoner until she had her own clothes back. She scanned the room, but saw nothing that looked like it might hold her clothes. Her eyes caught on a word printed on a flyer in a holder on the door. *Bellingham Wing.* The rest of the words she could see held no particular meaning, but something about those two words was special. She knew those words, but what they signified stayed out of her reach.

She tried to remember any hospitals near home, but came up empty. Not surprising. Something may come later. Once she was out in the world, things would come back.

Where would they keep her clothes? Or any clothes. Maybe she could steal a nurse's uniform from some closet, like they always did on television shows. How would she get home? She had no car keys. She didn't know of any bus stops near home. She'd have to call a cab.

Was she in the same city? She remembered the time she woke up in Atlanta and the housemaid whose southern accent was so thick she could not understand half of what she said. She'd had no money, and had to hitchhike back to the west coast.

She squinted, trying to read the smaller print on the flyers on the door. Montgomery General, she finally made out, half by guessing. Not a hospital she remembered.

If she could get to her own clothes, and maybe her own purse, she would have money. She always hid money in her clothing after Atlanta. The safe deposit box in Santa Barbara had extra credit cards. She could get a new license at the DMV if there wasn't one in her purse. If she had a phone or a computer, she could have her bank send a check by mail, if she had that much time. And an address. The computer didn't need a card or an ID, just a password.

She relaxed, and tried to sink back into the bed again. Someone would come along soon, and start asking questions. The questions would give her information. They will expect her to ask her own questions. She'd ask questions that gave nothing away, and just collect information. Give them nothing to raise suspicions.

In the meantime, she needed to go back to sleep, so the debilitating pressure waves behind her eyes could stop making it so hard to think.

~

A Distant Beacon

Walter Hastings walked into the day room and smiled. The television, mounted high on the wall, was replaying highlights of yesterday's episode of the day nurse's favorite soap opera.

"I know why she killed him," Walter said to no one. "She talks in her sleep."

He grinned again, and looked around the empty room. He was the first one there.

"Smartest guy in the room," he said, and grinned again.

The day room in the Bellingham Wing of Montgomery General was well appointed. There was a table set out with coffee urns and a pitcher of orange juice, and a wicker basket full of muffins, wrapped in a large blue table napkin. Walter lifted the corner of the napkin. Bran muffins today. He preferred the blueberry ones, but he took out a bran muffin anyway, and poured himself a glass of orange juice.

He buttoned the top button of his lab coat so that he wouldn't get crumbs or juice on his tie, and took the food over to a low table in front of the couch, where he could watch the television while he ate. The day nurse had given him the lab coat when the medicine had made it hard to drink without spilling. But that was back when the medicine had side effects. The new medicine was much better, and came in little orange flavored pills he could just chew.

He finished the muffin and juice and stood up to shake any crumbs away as he unbuttoned the lab coat. The soap opera had started, but the day nurse would start the recording over at the beginning. Walter changed the channel to a news station, then another, until he found one that was talking about news he cared about.

Wilson Bellingham, the man who named the wing of the hospital for himself, was still missing. Walter only cared because of the name. It was important to have anchors, and familiar names allowed him to correlate the things he saw happening around him. Names linked things, and let him know what was real. The hospital was real. Wilson Bellingham was real, because they had named the hospital after him.

There was a knock at the door. There should not have been a knock at the door, since the door was open. Things like that were clues that maybe something wasn't real. Walter looked over at the door, and confirmed that what he saw was almost certainly not real.

"Excuse me," said the man who had knocked. "I'm detective Reynolds," he said, pulling away his jacket to show the badge on his belt. "I was told Alice Watkins could be found here?"

"She'll be along shortly," Walter said, playing along. "How can Montgomery General assist the police department?"

"I don't mean to disturb you doctor, I just need to speak to Ms. Watkins," the detective said.

"No trouble at all," Walter said. "Help yourself to some coffee while you wait. Like I said, she'll be along shortly." He waved to the coffee urns on the table. "It's French Roast," Walter said. "I'm not a coffee drinker, but I'm told it is quite good."

Reynolds walked over to the table and inspected the coffee cups, glanced at the clock on the wall, and at the television still going on about the missing hedge fund manager, and after a bit of reflection, decided to pour himself a cup.

"Are you here about the Bellingham affair?" Walter asked, pointing to the television.

Reynolds looked up at the screen and studied it for a moment. "No, that'd be Missing Persons," he said. "I'm Homicide."

A Distant Beacon

"He's our benefactor, you know," Walter said. He gestured at the room and by implication the entire wing. "All of this, paid for by Bellingham. But you'll learn all about that when this case arrives at your desk. It really isn't just a Missing Persons case, you know."

"You saying someone killed him?" The detective asked, looking at Walter with narrowed eyes.

"Oh, I'm quite sure of it," Walter said, trying to remember all of the plot twists in the soap opera. "She's here in the hospital, you know, in this very wing. And she talks in her sleep," he added conspiratorially.

"Who does?" Reynolds asked.

"Mrs. Bellingham," Walter said.

"His wife," the detective confirmed, examining Walter closely. "And she talked in her sleep and said she killed him."

"Oh, not in so many words," Walter said. "That would make your job far too easy. But all of the clues are there; you just have to put them together. I'm sure you will, when it comes across your desk."

He moved closer to the detective. "I have learned from some of the best minds," he said. "Reality is subjective. What you see through your window onto life is not the whole story."

Alice Watkins interrupted him by walking into the room. The day nurse wore a clean white uniform with large pockets in front, into which she had thrust her hands. She seemed startled to see the detective and a bit anxious when she saw the badge.

"Ms. Watkins," Walter said graciously, "I'd like you to meet detective Reynolds." He gestured at the detective. "He has some things he'd like to discuss with you." He turned to the detective. "Shall I leave you two alone? It's a beautiful day for a walk in our gardens," he said, gesturing out at the greenery beyond the glass wall, and walking towards the glass door.

"Sure," the detective said, eyeing Walter with a puzzled expression. "You and I can talk later."

"When the case reaches your desk," Walter said with a polite smile on his face. "I'll look forward to your next visit." He let the door close behind him with a soft click as it latched. *I'm going to miss these interesting people if the pills work.* The thought made him sad.

Reynolds saw the expression on Alice's face, and began to put her at ease. "This is all routine stuff," he said. "You're not in any trouble. I just need to follow up with witnesses to the incident at McLaren's last night. You're on my list of patrons that were there, and I have some questions I need to ask, really, just routine things."

Alice relaxed just a little, and the detective gestured to the couch and sat down himself. Alice sat down a moment later, at the far end, her hands moving in the big pockets of her uniform.

"Did you know Mr. Wallace?" he asked. "Some of the other patrons said they thought you came in together."

"No," Alice said. "I think he might have come in behind me or something, but I don't know him." Her hands balled into fists inside the pockets.

"But you were talking to him just before the incident, is that correct?" he said, looking at his notes.

"Um," Alice said, hesitating. "I think he was hitting on all of the girls there," she said.

A Distant Beacon

The detective glanced up. "Mrs. Thompson and Mrs. Dane?" he asked. He scanned at his notes again. "They would seem to be a little, um, old for that, don't you think? Or were there other women there that I should be looking for?"

Alice looked down into her lap. "I think there might have been, maybe earlier."

"Don't worry," the detective said. "Like I said, this is just routine stuff. We have the guy who shot him in custody; he won't be coming after any witnesses or anything."

She didn't relax, and he tried again, standing up. "Can I get you some coffee?" he said, walking towards the table with the muffins and orange juice. "It really is quite good. Or some juice, maybe?"

"Coffee," she said. "Black, please." She stayed frozen in place at the end of the couch. Reynolds poured a cup of coffee for her, and refilled his own cup, stopping to add cream and sugar. He brought both cups back to the couch, handing her cup to her gently, and then sitting down closer than he had before. He took a noisy sip of the coffee before continuing.

"The assailant was seen to take something from the deceased after the shooting. Do you have any idea what it might have been? He didn't take the man's wallet, watch, or anything, but several witnesses report that he grabbed something from either the man's hand or his coat pocket. Did you get a chance to see what it might have been?"

"No," Alice said again, before putting her face into the coffee cup.

"No problem," the detective said. "It's just that you were apparently the closest person to Mr. Wallace just before the incident, and you probably had the best view. But don't worry, it's not that critical, we're just trying to establish motive, and tie up some loose ends."

Alice looked up at him. "What loose ends?" she asked.

"Nothing special," the detective said. "Mr. Wallace just seems to have no record of employment we can find. I was hoping to find out where he worked, to see if this could have been a workplace related incident. But that's a long shot. Wallace was well-dressed, expensive shoes, and all that, and the guy we took out of the hospital looks more like a bum, hadn't bathed in weeks. They can't have worked together."

"The hospital?" Alice asked.

"Yeah, he screwed up the getaway. Crashed his heap into the back of a patrol car and shot himself in the crotch. Not his day. No serious injuries, just some powder burns in sensitive areas, the whole squad got a big kick out of that. There's a reason they invented holsters. And safeties." The detective put his cup down on the low table.

"But they didn't find what he took from Jack?" Alice asked. "I mean Mr. Wallace."

"No sign of anything. A plastic bag, but it was empty. They're testing it for drugs; he might have been dumb enough to swallow the evidence. This guy isn't the quickest bunny in the forest." The detective stood up again.

"So, to recap," he said, looking at his notes, "you don't know Mr. Wallace, you think he came in just after you, he chatted you up, and maybe some other women not on the list, and you didn't see what was taken from the deceased. Is there anything you can think of to add to our investigation?"

"I don't think so," Alice said.

A Distant Beacon

"Well then," Reynolds said, extending his hand to help her up from the couch. "It's been a pleasure chatting with you, I'm sorry to take so much of your time, I know how busy nurses can be."

Alice nodded, and the detective let himself out.

Once in his car, Reynolds made a phone call. "Watch her house," he said, "she's definitely involved. Probably knows both of them."

In the day room, Alice took the cups to the sink and rinsed them before loading them into the tray to for washing. She saw Walter's back through the window, where he had stayed throughout the entire conversation with the detective. She then quickly left the room, heading for the ladies' room.

Once there, she checked each of the stalls, and seeing they were all empty, entered the one on the end, bolting the metal door behind her. She got out her cell phone and speed dialed a number.

"It's me," she said. "A cop showed up here, asking about last night. Jack is dead, and that idiot Marvin sent to take care of things is in jail. He ran into a cop car and then nearly shot his dick off with the gun he used on Jack."

She listened for a while. "No, he just asked some dumb questions and left. He's just going through the motions. There's nothing to tie us into it, even if he gives up Marvin."

She listened again. "I have some more. They changed it though, this time it says to take two of them, so they might have cut the dose. I'll test it out in a minute."

Someone else came into the restroom, and Alice pressed her finger on the phone to end the call. She waited until she was alone again, and then stood up and got one of the capsules out of her pocket. She opened it carefully, and closed one nostril as she brought half the capsule up to the other and took a strong sniff.

Her screams echoed down the hallway, and several people came running into the room to find her at the sink, flushing her face with water.

~

A Distant Beacon

Doctor Thomas Williams sat in front of the big desk that hospital administrator Ethel Harris sat behind. He was familiar with being in this situation, but he was relaxed and unshaken, knowing that his place in the organization was secure, having been responsible for the funding of the entire Bellingham Wing. He was nonetheless polite and responsive to the administrator's questions.

"I presume you have some idea about why Nurse Alice Watkins was cursing your name and screaming in the ladies' room earlier this morning?"

"I have a good idea," Williams said.

"And you're going to share that idea with me?" Harris continued.

"Ms. Watkins might prefer that I didn't," Williams replied.

"Is there something going on between you two?" she asked.

"Good lord, no," Williams said, almost laughing. "Nothing like that."

"Spill," Harris said.

"You won't like it," he said.

"I already don't like it," she answered, and waited.

"I was concerned about Walter Hastings," Williams said. "He wasn't responding to the new medication. Neither in a positive way, nor in a negative way, by which I mean the side effects we would normally expect at that dosage."

He paused, and she waited for him to continue.

"Anyway, I noticed that nurse Watkins was displaying some of the side effects we were expecting to see in Mr. Hastings. Her cognitive state was difficult to determine from visual observation, but she had the eyelid droop and the quiver in the lip we expect to see in patients on PSD-231. But I became certain of it when Walter thanked me for making the pills orange flavored. I hadn't." Williams sat back in his chair and waited for Harris to reply.

"Correct procedure would be to notify me," she said, "and we would notify the police."

"But she's far too good a nurse to lose," Williams said. "And Trauma Induced Avoidance Therapy works so well in rats and lower primates."

Harris closed her eyes and sank back into her chair. "What did you do, Thomas?" she asked in a quiet voice.

"I had the pharmacy change the formula," he said. "From one milligram to half a milligram per capsule. And to change the label to two pills daily instead of one. And to fill the rest of the capsule with 100% capsaicin."

"You put pepper spray in a patient's PSD-231 capsules?" Harris asked.

"It has mild mood altering properties. It is often prescribed in capsule form for the treatment of several of Hastings' symptoms," Williams offered.

"You do realize we could be sued," Harris said.

"I doubt it," Williams said. "PSD-231 will only get someone high if it is snorted. Delivered nasally, I mean. In this instance, she certainly delivered it in that fashion, contrary to the labeling. But Ms. Watkins was not the patient, and she stole the drugs. I don't think she is going to pursue this matter in the courts."

"And in the meantime?" Harris asked.

A Distant Beacon

"I expect she will become a model employee," Williams said. "She's very good at what she does, and she is a very quick learner."

Chapter Two

Nurse Watkins was already in the day room when Walter arrived. She had her tray of little paper cups with pills, each one a different color, with a different patient's name printed on the bottom. She turned to face him when she heard his footsteps behind her.

"You have new meds," she said, picking up his blue paper cup. She sounded congested, and her eyes and nose had the red look of someone with a sinus problem. "You need to take two now, and make *sure* to take them on a full stomach," she said, placing particular emphasis on the word *sure*.

She left in a hurry, not stopping to chat as she usually did. The television was not on, which was also unusual. He wondered if she would come back to watch the soap opera with him as she usually did. Somehow, he suspected today was special.

"You might want to have the kitchen make you a couple soft boiled eggs," a voice said behind him.

Walter knew the voice wasn't real. There was no such thing as a talking alpaca. But George's advice was never wrong, and he had learned to benefit from it. He turned around, and the familiar fuzzy white face looked him in the eye. "And a glass of milk might be a good idea as well."

Walter stared into his blue cup at the two large capsules and knew he was going to miss the tiny little chewable orange pills. He left the day room, and started walking towards the kitchen.

"All that stuff in there is basically just sugar," George said. "Even the orange juice. You're better off eating the whole orange, and not just squeezing the sugar water part into a glass. And serving cake for breakfast, those blueberry things you like, this is a hospital, and they ought to know better."

A Distant Beacon

Walter didn't answer, because he knew George wasn't real. George never minded when Walter ignored him. Alpacas were patient. Even imaginary talking alpacas. At least Walter imagined they were. He had never actually met any besides George.

When his eggs were ready, Walter considered putting butter and salt on them, but one look at George and he simply carried his bowl of eggs and his glass of milk over to the big table in the dining area.

Jimmy Dingle was already there, finishing a bowl of soft-boiled eggs and a glass of milk. Walter was pretty sure Jimmy Dingle wasn't real, but other people talked to Jimmy as if they could see him too, so he wasn't quite sure. But Jimmy talked about things that couldn't be real, and did things like ordering the same thing as you did, but before he could know what you were ordering, like the soft-boiled eggs.

"It's the new meds," Jimmy said, pointing to his empty bowl of eggs. "You have to take them on a full stomach. And whole milk helps, not the nonfat stuff. You should put butter on those," he said, pointing to Walter's eggs. Walter glanced over at George, but George had an expression that looked like he would have shrugged his shoulders if he could have. Walter decided to have butter on his eggs tomorrow.

"Your friend will be awake today," Jimmy said. "But she won't know you, because she's someone else now. So don't get upset, and don't call her Cordelia, she'll get mad if you do, and she needs her friends."

Jimmy was always talking like that, as if he knew the future like it had just happened. To him it just had. He was convinced that he was living his life backwards, and could not remember yesterday because he hadn't lived it yet. But he could remember the part of today that hadn't happened yet. And he was really good at predicting things, but really bad about doing anything about them.

Walter said nothing, since he didn't think Jimmy was real. He just put his spoon into his eggs and began cutting them up into little pieces. Doctor Williams brought his tray over and sat down next to him.

"Hello Walter," the doctor said. "Good morning Jimmy." Walter looked from Jimmy to the doctor and back, then took a spoonful of eggs, nodding towards the doctor.

"I should have had butter," Walter said, looking at the doctor.

"She's not going to take it well," Jimmy said to Williams.

"Is that right?" the doctor said. Walter could not tell which of them he was speaking to.

"But I have whole milk," Walter said, watching the doctor out of the corner of his eye.

"Just a head's up," Jimmy said, standing up and lifting his tray to leave. "She's not the person she was."

"That's good," the doctor said. Walter still could not tell whom he was addressing. Sometimes the doctor pretended to talk to George, even when George wasn't there, and wasn't real even when he was there. It was to find out if Walter was taking his pills. Walter finished the last of his eggs, and made a show of tipping his pills into his hands and washing them down with the last of his milk.

The doctor didn't seem to notice. "We're taking Cordelia off the drip this morning," he said to Walter. "She'll probably want to see her friends, if you'd like to drop by, maybe in the afternoon. She'll still be a bit groggy, and she'll be taking something for the

A Distant Beacon

headaches, but a bit of company might be just what the doctor ordered," he said, grinning at his joke.

Walter didn't mention what Jimmy had said. But he nodded at the doctor. "She needs her friends," he said, echoing what Jimmy had told him.

"Indeed, she does," Williams said. "We all do, don't we?" He winked, and Walter wondered if he had meant Jimmy or George. But he was done with his breakfast, and he stood up to leave, wondering if Nurse Watkins had started watching the soap opera in the day room.

"People who do bad things should learn not to talk in their sleep," Walter said to Williams. The doctor looked at him, surprised at first, and then remembered who was speaking.

"Sage advice, as always," he said, and made a mock salute with one finger to his temple.

~

When Sarah woke up again, the tubing had been removed from her wrist, and her headache seemed even worse than it had been earlier. The dressing on her head had been changed, and the wires were gone. So too was the pulse monitor on her finger.

Attempting to sit up caused more pounding in her head, so she rolled over onto her stomach, and lowered one leg gingerly to the floor. The floor, like everything else in the room, was cold, and her head hurt again when she jerked her foot up at the contact. But she put her foot back down, and gently swung the other leg around to join it, and rose slowly, her hands on the bed for balance. The pressure behind her eyes brought momentary tunnel vision, and tears rolled down her face, but she stood still, and the pain became manageable again.

She did not trust herself to walk. The back of the hospital gown was undone, and she lifted her hands from the bed to tie it back. She steadied herself by pressing one leg against the bed. She felt dizzy for a moment, and looked around for something to throw up in, but the feeling passed.

She felt the bandages on her head. She could tell that her head had not been shaved, and she felt some relief at that. But the nature of her injuries was a mystery. There were some sore spots under the bandages, but they were localized, so a skull fracture was unlikely. She checked the rest of her body for bruises or any other signs of an accident, but found no other injury.

Nail polish, she noted. She never wore colored nail polish, and seldom even clear polish. But these nails were carefully manicured, bright scarlet with pearl tips. But the last bit of polish was a distance from the cuticle, indicating it had been at least a week, maybe two, since they had been done.

Edging herself along the bed, she took unsteady steps towards the only reading matter in the room, the rack of fliers to the side of the

A Distant Beacon

door. She took the one that had *Bellingham Wing* printed on it, and began to read.

Mental rehabilitation. Recovery and convalescence. Dealing with drug side effects. Psychotherapy. Group therapy. Dialing in your dosage. Asking for help.

"I'm in a nut house," she said aloud. It might be harder to leave than she had expected. She thought about the best way to overcome a guard and steal his clothes, but noticed that her once-toned body did not feel as strong as it should have. *How long have I been here?*

Her fingernails said she hadn't been there long enough to lose muscle tone. *How long has it been this time?*

There was a knock at the door, and the handle started to turn. Sarah jumped at the sound, the pain in her head brought more tunnel vision, and she sat back down on the bed quickly. She had just brought her breathing back under control when a tall man entered the room, wearing a white shirt and tie under his white lab coat.

"Oh, excellent, I see you're up," he said. "How's the head?"

She considered her words carefully before answering. *Don't give anything away. Should I know this guy?*

"About what you'd expect," she said.

"Oh dear," he replied. "That bad, eh? Well I brought some of the good stuff with me. Some for the pain and some for the inflammation, which should also help with the pain."

He held out a small yellow paper cup and a glass of water. In the cup were two small pills, and two larger capsules.

"Which is which?" she asked, and then immediately regretted it. But the doctor did not seem to notice.

"The little ones are the good stuff," he said, winking. "The big ones just reduce the swelling."

She took the cup, holding it in her hand so that he could not see it, and reached for the glass of water as she palmed the small pills and let the larger ones fall back into the cup. She flipped the contents of the cup into her mouth with a quick flourish that brought stabbing blindness once again, and washed them down with the water, draining the cup. The room came back into view a moment later, and she slid her hand secretly under the sheet, leaving the small pills behind.

The doctor was walking towards the window. "Do you think you can handle a little sunlight?" he asked. "A bright room is a happy room." He opened the curtains before she could answer, and she squinted. It hurt her head to squint, but she said nothing, allowing her eyes to adjust.

"We won't know for sure until we do the fMRI, but the procedure went well, everything looks good. We'll want to start the exercises as soon as possible, to avoid losing anything. The extra plasticity means you'll learn new things quickly, but we don't want you losing anything along the way."

"We don't want to lose anything," she echoed, wondering what that meant. It sounded ominous, but she recognized she was in a somewhat paranoid frame of mind. Paranoia was good, it kept you safe.

"Nosirree," the doctor said, grinning.

"I'd like to get dressed," Sarah said, choosing her words carefully.

A Distant Beacon

"All your things are in your recovery room," the doctor said. "You shouldn't wash your hair until tomorrow morning, and you should be careful around the entry points, but there's a shower cap in the bathroom for you. I expect you're starving. I can have a light lunch brought to your room, something that won't upset your stomach."

"That would be nice," she said.

There was another knock at the door, and, as before, the door opened without any pause after the knock.

"Ah, good," the doctor said, looking at the woman who entered the room. "Nurse Watkins will help you over to your recovery suite. I'll have a wheelchair brought around."

Sarah considered this, and then said, "I think I'd like to try walking," she began, stopping herself as she had almost asked how far away 'recovery' was. He might expect her to know.

"Feeling that chipper, eh? That's great news. Our first one just wanted to go back to sleep right away."

Sarah took the nurse's hand, reaching her other hand under the sheet as if to steady herself, while palming the pills there. She stood up slowly, and the edges of her vision went black again. She controlled her breathing so the two would not know how much pain she was in, and took a step forward, leaning heavily on the nurse. Together, they made their way out the door, and turned right. The doctor watched from the corridor for a moment, and then said, "I'll have an orderly bring you your lunch," before they turned the corner and could see him no longer.

A few steps down the hallway, the nurse whispered in Sarah's ear. "That man is pure evil," she said. "Don't trust him." Sarah looked into the woman's face, noting the reddened nose and eyes, as if the woman had been crying. She tightened her grip on the woman's hand for a moment in camaraderie.

Once in the recovery room, which turned out to be only a few yards from the room she had awakened in, the nurse led Sarah to a large bed with a bright yellow bedspread and half a dozen big pillows, and left her leaning against it as she walked to the curtains and spread them wide. Late morning sunlight filled the room, and Sarah could see into three other well-appointed rooms as the nurse walked into each and opened more curtains.

This place is bigger than my whole house.

The nurse walked back into the room and opened a large closet. "All your things are here," she said, waving a hand towards the interior. "And in here," she said, indicating a large dresser to the side of the bed.

"And just between you and me," she said, "the opiates work a *lot* better with some help from the wet bar in the living room. There's some 15 year old single malt in there we had to hide from the orderlies. Look under the ice bucket."

She winked conspiratorially. "Doctor Williams probably ordered you something like oatmeal for lunch," she said, making a face. "But the chef grills a mean rib-eye if you'd rather eat something real. I can tell him to bring one up if you'd like."

Sarah smiled weakly, pressing her leg against the bed for balance. "Oatmeal will be fine, I think," she said. "But thanks," she added, her voice a bit lower, acknowledging her newfound conspirator.

"I'll leave you to freshen up then," the nurse said. "Unless you'd like help into the shower?"

"I'll be fine," Sarah lied, feeling dizzy. When the nurse left, closing the door behind her, Sarah slid slowly onto the bed, turning onto

A Distant Beacon

her side to lower herself down, so as not to cause her head to explode again.

She awoke to a knock at the door. This time, it did not open. There was another quiet, very polite knock. Sarah slid her legs onto the floor slowly, and pushed herself upright. "Come in," she said.

A young man in jeans and sneakers under his white coat came in, pushing a steam cart with covered dishes on it. There was a single rose in a vase on the cart next to the place setting.

"I'll put this in the dining room if that's all right," he said, not looking directly at her in her hospital gown.

"That would be great," Sarah said.

He clattered away in the other room for a minute or two, and then pushed the cart back to the entryway.

"Um," Sarah said, before he could leave. He stopped and glanced back at her, then dropped his eyes to the floor between them.

"Yes, Mrs. Bellingham?" he said.

She paused at the name, and then forged ahead. "What did they tell you about, um, all this?" she asked, trying to remember just how she had planned to say the words.

"They don't tell us much," he said. "Patient confidentiality and all that. Or did you mean about your husband?" he asked.

That caught Sarah by surprise. She wasn't married. Couldn't possibly be married.

"I've been out of it for a bit," she said carefully. "Tell me everything you know."

"Well, they still can't find him. The stock is tanking, and it's in all the papers. We're not supposed to tell anyone you're here, of course, but they're saying both of you probably went off somewhere, and maybe there was a plane crash or something." He paused, looking at the floor.

"Hey," she said softly. "It's just us two here, you can talk to me."

He met her eyes, and then quickly looked down again. She saw his discomfort, and glanced over at the open closet.

"Could you bring me that robe?" she asked, pointing to the closet.

He rushed over to bring it to her, and faced the other way as she put it on and sat back down slowly.

"You're such a gentleman," she said, and he turned back around, meeting her gaze this time.

"What do you know about why I'm here?" she asked.

"You mean, like, why this whole place was built just for you? I know they have a lot of other patients, but they built this whole wing just to help you get better. Is that what you mean?" he asked.

She held her face in a poker smile, hard as that was. "Did they tell you what I was getting better from?" she asked.

"No ma'am," he said.

She sensed he wanted to be anywhere but here right now.

"I should let you go," she said. "But do you think you could maybe come by for a chat later? Catch me up on all the gossip around this place? You must know a lot about everything that goes on here. And I'm just nuts about gossip," she said, regretting the word immediately, considering her surroundings.

A Distant Beacon

"I guess so," he said. "I'll probably be bringing your dinner later."

"Wonderful," she said. "Bring two; we can chat over some rib-eyes and cocktails. I won't tell anyone."

He nodded and left as quickly as the cart would let him manage it through the door.

Sarah stood up carefully, and made her way into the huge bathroom. The shower was a large walk-in space made of glass bricks. She examined herself in the mirror before putting on the shower cap she found on the counter, and started the shower.

The hot water felt great after the cold hospital room, and she lingered for a long time, letting the water run over her. The towels she found when she got out of the shower were the most amazing that she had ever felt, and they had been embroidered with the monogram CB.

What kind of hospital is this?

She examined herself in the mirror. Her body was still toned and slim, muscled in the right places from all the time she put in at the gym, but softer than she remembered. She removed the shower cap and examined the bandages. She could not tell what damage there was. But the steamy shower and the anti-inflammatories had helped to relieve the pressure in her head.

Returning to the bedroom, she entered the closet to find some jeans and a T-shirt to put on. She found nothing that appeared casual. Several of the pieces in the closet looked like they would need assistance putting on, and double-stick tape to stay on. She was no judge of fabric or style, but everything in the closet looked like it belonged to a movie star, not a waitress.

She settled on the simplest outfit she could find, a simple blouse and a tailored pair of slacks. There were dozens of shoes, and she searched for a pair she thought she could run in should the need arise, but settled for a pair she felt she might walk in without pain. Everything fit her body perfectly.

If they know me so well, where is my guitar?

In the dining room, the oatmeal had gone cold. A cloth napkin had been folded into an intricate shape, and the rose placed in front of the plate. She walked into a kitchen, where there was a large refrigerator, oven, stove, and a microwave oven, as if someone was actually living here. She got the oatmeal from the dining room and warmed it up in the microwave, eating it from the bowl as she walked around the recovery suite. She had been hungry. It had only been masked by the headache.

She opened the drapes in the living room, and discovered she had a view of the Pacific Ocean from what she decided was at least seven stories above the cliffs below. She could see a road winding around the building, but no traffic. The glass doors opened at her touch, sliding silently into the walls, and the sea breeze entered the room. She walked out onto a large balcony, surrounded by high glass walls. The sun felt warm on her face behind the glass, and the fresh air was a welcome change after the sterile hospital.

There was a knock at the door behind her, and she carried the empty bowl back into the suite, and opened the door herself.

A man stood at the door, dressed neatly in a pressed shirt and tie, a white lab coat unbuttoned over it. He waited for her to say something, his eyes scanning the bandages on her head, her clothes, her shoes, but always somehow back to her eyes just at the right time.

"Yes?" she said.

"Should I introduce myself?" Walter asked, politely.

A Distant Beacon

"That's usually a good start," Sarah said, but something in his eyes told her that was exactly the wrong thing to say. She was supposed to know this person. "But in your case, of course, not necessary. But go ahead and try it anyway."

He glanced to his left, as if someone out of sight in the hallway had just spoken. Sarah moved slightly to get a better view in that direction, but there was no one there.

"Jimmy said you wouldn't know me," Walter said. "And George says you definitely don't know me. But Jimmy said you would need your friends, and not to call you Cordelia. So, I'm here. I'm Walter Hastings. We're friends. We do the crossword puzzle together in the mornings, and you help me know who is real and who isn't."

She could tell that something was not quite right with Walter Hastings. *You're in a mental hospital with bandages on your head. He's just missing the bandages.*

He was not a large man, and she felt sure she could handle him if anything got physical. And he seemed to have information, and that is what she needed more than anything else.

"Come on in," she said.

"You look like her," he said, entering the room and walking in a familiar way into the living room. He sat down at the end of the large couch, his body angled toward the smaller couch at right angles to it, as if he expected her to sit there. She did.

"But she's much more soignée. She'd never wear those things together," he said.

She looked down at her clothes and shoes. She was going to ask what was wrong with them, but kept her questions. He seemed quite content to do all the talking, and she was not comfortable confirming his suspicions until she knew more about what was going on here.

Choosing her words carefully, she said, "Do you know who is real and who isn't right now?"

"You're real," he said. "You just aren't Cordelia. George isn't real, but he is too useful to ignore. I'm never sure about Jimmy. Other people see him, but he can't really know what's going to happen."

"What do you know about this place?" Sarah asked.

"You mean the Bellingham Wing," Walter said, after some initial uncertainty. "It's nice. Much better than other places I've been. That's because you built it for you. I mean Cordelia built it for herself, even if it's named for her husband. Are you Theresa? She told me about Theresa, and someone else, but I forget her name." He stopped and looked at Sarah, expecting her help with the other name. Sarah said nothing.

Walter seemed to realize something. "You're the other one," he said. "Cordelia said you didn't know about the others. Oh, wow, you have no idea why you're here. Doctor Williams thinks you're still Cordelia. He'll be totally panicked if he thinks he's screwed this up."

Walter stopped talking and stared at Sarah intently, then put his hand on hers. She resisted the urge to pull away. "You *are* real, aren't you?" he asked.

The question took Sarah by surprise. *Answer with a question.* "Would I tell you if I weren't?" she asked.

"George would," Walter said, suddenly no longer concerned. "He's always reminding me he doesn't exist. But he's a talking alpaca, so it's always pretty easy with him." Then his expression

A Distant Beacon

changed again, this time triumphant. "Morganna," he said. "That was the other one. Are you Morganna?"

"Do you want me to be?" Sarah asked.

"You don't want Doctor Williams to know, do you?" Walter said, in a way that made it clear it was not a question. "I won't tell. I know Cordelia said she'd still be there after all the personalities merged back together. I think we all just assumed she'd be the one who woke up."

He stopped talking, and the two of them sat there, looking at one another. Both were processing the information between them, but in different ways. Walter was the first to break the silence.

"OK, now remember that I have disintegration disorder, so I can't really promise that everything I know is really true. If something doesn't seem to make sense, I can usually figure it out, but sometimes things *seem* to make sense and I can't tell. But I'll try to fill you in, OK?"

"Sure," Sarah said, still wary. "But first tell me what disintegration disorder is."

"I dream while I'm awake," Walter said. "It makes it really hard to tell if something is really happening, or if I'm dreaming it. If I watch television, the people in the shows sometimes sit next to me and ask me things. Or if I need advice, George will say something. Doctor Williams thinks that the pills will help, but so far they just make me sleepy."

"So you think you might be dreaming all of this," Sarah said.

"Probably not," Walter said. "Except for George. I never learn new things from the dream parts; it's always stuff I already know."

"I'm real," Sarah said.

"You're just not Cordelia," Walter said, nodding. "OK, so here's what I know. Cordelia figured out there were others. She found out about Theresa first, and left notes for Theresa so they could figure out how not to keep screwing each other up."

"They set things up so that someone would always be watching, and take care of whoever woke up, and do things like pay the bills and stuff."

"Then Cordelia learned about the cure, but it only worked on mice and monkeys. But Cordelia is married to Wilson Bellingham, so she has lots of money and can make things happen. She hired Doctor Williams because she thought he was the kind of person who wouldn't mind doing human trials right away. And she bought the old hospital and added this wing, and brought in all of us nut jobs so Doctor Williams would have cover. And even after the first guy they tried it on didn't work out that well, they went ahead and tried it on her next. On you."

Walter took a deep breath and let it back out. Sarah's eyes narrowed a bit as she asked her next question. "What happened to the first guy?"

"He kind of forgot who he was," Walter said. "Nice guy, really sharp, could do all kinds of things. Doctor Wilson said he figured out what the problem was, and made up some exercises so that it wouldn't happen to anyone else."

"He forgot who he was?" Sarah asked.

"Not like you not knowing about Cordelia," Walter said. "He forgot all of them. He woke up as one of them, but then just forgot after a while."

A Distant Beacon

There was a knock at the door, and it swung open before Sarah could say anything. Nurse Watkins walked in, carrying a tray full of paper cups, each one a different color.

"Oh, hello Walter," she said, seeing them together on the couch. "You shouldn't be bothering Mrs. Bellingham, she needs her rest." She set the tray down on the low table where Sarah had put her feet, and picked up a yellow paper cup.

"These are for you, dear," she said to Sarah, handing her the cup. She examined the other cups for a moment, and then picked up the blue one. "Here are yours," she said to Walter, studying his face as if expecting to find something that wasn't there. She glanced back down into the blue cup and then back up at Walter. "Make sure to take them on a full stomach," she said in a low voice.

She turned to Sarah again. "Shall I get you a glass of water?" she asked. "Or maybe something with ice?" she hinted, as if they shared a secret.

"I'm fine, thanks," Sarah said, picking up the cup. She started for the kitchen.

"OK Walter," the nurse said, taking his hand and walking him towards the door. "Let's get you a snack down in the kitchen."

Sarah looked over at Walter, who smiled and winked back at her before following the nurse out the door. The door closed behind them.

Sarah gazed into the cup for a while, then took out the two large capsules, and tipped the smaller pills into the sink. She ran the water, took a handful of it into her mouth, and followed it with the capsules. She swallowed, took another handful of water, swallowed again, and wiped her mouth on her sleeve.

Somehow, she knew that Cordelia Bellingham would never put her feet on the furniture, drink from the faucet, or wipe her mouth on her shirtsleeve. It made her feel good to know she wasn't that person. She tried to belch noisily, but only ended up making her head hurt. It was time to lie down and try to sleep the headache off again.

Just how much do you want to believe some certified nut case who talks to imaginary friends and admits he doesn't know what is real?

Chapter Three

Jonas Reynolds nursed his beer, trying to hear what his partner was saying over the din of the television and the other patrons in the bar. He didn't care much for beer, but found that holding one in his hand kept people from trying to get him to drink. He liked to keep his head clear, and he could nurse a single beer for most of an evening in this kind of social situation.

"All these people complaining that the guy is missing, but no one has a decent photo of him? How do you get to be a gazzilionaire if you never meet people face-to-face?" David Archer was on his fifth or sixth beer, and didn't seem to have Reynolds' need for mental clarity.

"Internet," Reynolds almost shouted. "They say he does everything by email."

Archer seemed to turn this thought around in his head for a while, trying to get a firm grasp on a slippery concept. "So maybe it's just that his cable is out," he said, finding his joke especially funny. He giggled at his brilliance for a while as the news station continued its coverage of Wilson Bellingham's disappearance.

"That's not right," Reynolds said, half to Archer and half to the television. "His wife isn't missing, she's at Montgomery General."

"Where'd you hear that?" Archer asked, his face turning into a caricature of puzzlement. "Carlisle's been looking for the lady for a week now, got bupkis."

"A doctor there in the new wing, for the mental cases, told me she was staying there. Said she talked in her sleep about killing her husband." Reynolds put his beer to his lips, and pretended to drink.

"Did you tell Carlisle?" Archer wanted to know.

"Let him do his own legwork," Reynolds said, a look of distaste on his face. "The guy's a jerk. Were you there when he tried to blame Susie for the mess he made of that thing with the mayor's kid? A real class act."

"But you gotta say something," Archer said. "You can't withhold information."

"It's just hearsay. The guy said she didn't actually say she killed him, said that would make it too easy for the police. There's nothing there."

Archer disagreed. "He's looking for the wife, and we know where she is. This is high profile; it's all over the news. If she's hiding at the hospital, that doesn't seem weird to you? Nobody at the hospital speaks up, but a doctor there tells a cop she killed her husband just out of the blue?"

"You weren't there, man. He acted like it was no big deal, so I blew it off, it wasn't like he was tugging my arm and whispering in my ear, it was more like we were talking about the ball game." Reynolds did not like being questioned this way, but the more he thought about it, the more the drunken Archer seemed to make sense.

"You tell Carlisle," he said. "Just don't say it came from me. Say you heard it in the bar, which you did."

"From a reliable source," Archer said.

"From some guy with a beer in his hand," Reynolds said.

~

A Distant Beacon

Sarah awoke to a knock at the door, followed immediately by the sound of the door swinging open.

I wonder if the door has a lock?

Nurse Watkins entered the bedroom. "Today we take the bandages off," she said. "Then you get your fMRI, and start on the exercises." She seemed cheery today, and the puffy eyes and sniffle were gone.

She waited expectantly at the foot of the bed, and Sarah concluded that she was going to stay there until something changed.

"How about handing me my robe," Sarah said. It didn't matter that the nurse had seen it all before, she wasn't going to stand up naked and walk around in front of the woman.

Alice brought over the robe, and Sarah got into it discretely, holding it at her neck while she slipped her arms in, then standing up and letting the covers fall with the rest of the robe.

Her head no longer hurt, and standing up did not bring a ring of grey around her vision, or ringing in her ears. That was a good sign. She thought of how she could pump the nurse for information.

"Walter says he's disintegrating," she said.

The nurse laughed. "He has dis-integration disorder," she said, stressing the first syllable and spacing it from the rest of the word. It means he has trouble integrating."

"He dreams while he's awake," Sarah repeated.

"Exactly. He has these elaborate stories going on in his head all the time, and he *integrates* them with his real life so he can't tell which is which. He had me totally going one time, it all seemed to make so much sense, and then I found out it was the plot of the book he was reading." She reached for Sarah's chin to turn her head, and stuck an infrared thermometer in her ear. It beeped, and she recorded the reading on the electronic tablet she carried.

"So he's schizophrenic," Sarah said.

"No, they have good drugs for that. His problem is more like yours, but he can't afford the plasticity treatments you're getting. So he gets happy pills."

"He should have picked my health plan," Sarah said, trying to decide if the nurse was going to let her shower before taking her somewhere.

"We all need your health plan!" the nurse laughed. "That robe doesn't have any metal in it, right? It's probably OK to wear it for the fMRI."

"I think I'd rather be a little more dressed, if possible," Sarah said.

"Oh, OK, there are some pajamas in the dresser, with draw strings."

The nurse seemed content to watch her dress, but Sarah decided to take the pajamas into the bathroom. She brushed her teeth and rinsed her face, then donned the pajamas. Looking in the mirror and making a face, she decided to wear the robe over them.

The nurse led her to the elevator, and they descended several floors, and then walked for what seemed like several blocks past closed doors, with no one in sight.

"Busy place," Sarah said.

A Distant Beacon

Alice laughed. "We'll fill it up. It's all new right now, your wing. You'll get the bandages off in the main hospital, and the imaging center is there too."

The exited through double doors into a bustling hospital, with people seated in waiting areas off the main corridor. Alice led Sarah around a corner and down a hallway, and finally into a well-lit room with several people seated waiting their turns. The nurse ignored them, and led Sarah directly into an exam room, where another nurse waited.

"Candy is here to take the bandages off," Alice said. "I'll go prep the imaging room, and come back for you." She left the small room.

"Go ahead and sit down," Nurse Candy said, indicating the vinyl-clad bench with paper rolled over it. Sarah sat and the nurse brought over scissors and a stainless steel bowl.

"Oh, they did a nice job on these," she said, lifting the edge of the bandage. "No tape stuck to your hair, a nice bit of gauze cap, you must have made some friends somewhere." She busied herself cutting away the tape and gauze.

"Nothing shaved," she said, in a puzzled tone. "Oh, I see," she said immediately after. "All that for this little thing." She peeled away more bandage. "And a matching one on the other side. Nice little stitches, so tiny. What did you have done, dear? I've never seen anything like this."

"Actually," Sarah said, "I haven't a clue. What does it look like?"

"It's healed up nicely," the nurse said. "Just a couple little spots. I'd say you could wash your hair if you wanted to, just be careful here, and here," she said, gently brushing the hairs behind her ears on either side.

Sarah reached up and touched the spots, feeling the stitching. The spots were indeed tiny, as if she'd just had a mole removed. She felt no pain when she pressed on it.

The nurse brought out a comb and started running it lightly through Sarah's short hair.

"There you go, all pretty," she said. There was no mirror in the room to confirm the observation.

The nurse left, and Sarah waited in the room alone for about twenty minutes before Alice returned.

"Oh, that looks much better," she said, examining Sarah's head carefully from several vantage points. "They brought in a cosmetic surgeon from LA just to do those stitches for you," she said. "Real cutie pie, that guy. Too bad you slept right through it."

The imaging room was down another hundred feet of busy corridor, and past two sets of swinging doors. Doctor Wilson met her there.

"This will be just like the other times," he said. "A different set of questions, of course, but we're looking for the same kinds of things." He led her through another door as he spoke, and gestured to another vinyl-clad bench covered with paper, sticking out of a huge machine like a grey tongue.

"Stay very still," he said, adjusting pads around her head that made it impossible not to obey his stricture. "I'll be in the other room, like before, and you'll hear me through the speakers."

He left her lying on the paper, and after a few minutes, the grey tongue pulled back into the big machine, her head entering first. The machine began making very loud rhythmic banging sounds.

A Distant Beacon

"OK then," Williams' voice came from behind her head. "First I want you to try to picture yourself looking in a mirror. I'll shut up while you do that, so the verbal processing centers don't activate."

The machine banged away, and Sarah decided, what the hell, and pictured the bathroom, then the mirror, and the image of her bandaged head. She mentally removed the bandages, and imagined her hair the way she normally did it, long, parted well to her left, and draped over her right eye. Then she was in the bathroom at home, looking in the small medicine cabinet mirror, putting on eye makeup.

She heard Williams' voice again. "Now I'd like you to imagine driving your car," he said.

She pictured her little car, plugged into its charger in the garage, the red paint, and the cute little tires. She removed the cable, and got into the car, and the lights on the dash came on as she sat down. The garage door was open, and she backed out onto the street, and then drove to the corner. Without segue she was on the freeway, years ago, in a car with a gearshift and a noisy turbocharged engine.

"Fine," came the voice behind her. "Now picture your husband," it said.

Sarah frowned. Husband. There was absolutely no way she had a husband. She pictured several men, television personalities, politicians, Walter, Doctor Williams, and quickly rejected each of them. Husband. She'd never even had a boyfriend.

Something nagged at her. An image that would not take shape. She ignored it, and thought about driving again, on the freeway in the noisy car. She pressed her foot on the accelerator, and passed cars one after another, each with a fast "whoosh!' as she sped by.

She wove in and out of traffic, pushing her foot down hard on the pedal.

"And now, picture your mother," the voice said. Again, Sarah felt confused. She had no image of her mother. No motherly figures at all. She pictured mothers on television, lifting a child up to hold, making sandwiches in a kitchen. She pictured the Virgin Mary with a halo. However, no image of her mother came to her.

They messed up your head. The last guy forgot who he was. We don't want to lose anything.

Sarah tried to sit up, and struggled out of the confining machine. She could hear the doctor's voice calling from the speaker in the banging machine. "Please sit still, we're not done," he called, but she was standing up, and walking towards the door.

Williams met her on the other side. The banging behind the door had stopped, and it was quiet in the room, just the two of them standing face to face, the doctor blocking her path to the other door.

"I take it I'm not talking to Cordelia Bellingham," Williams said, reaching for her arm. She brushed his hand away.

"Please," he said. "Come sit, we can talk."

"What did you do to me?" Sarah said, anger supplanting her earlier wariness. "What the *fuck* did you do to my head!" She hit him in the shoulder with the palm of her hand, hard. He backed up a step.

"Theresa?" he asked. Getting no response, he tried again. "Morganna?"

"I want out of here," she said. "I'm going home."

A Distant Beacon

"You can't," Williams said. "You need to do the exercises. You need to integrate. It's the whole point of the procedure."

"So I can be like Walter?" she asked. "No thanks! Was he the first guy you tried this on? Is that why he's totally bonkers?" She pushed past him to get to the door.

"What?" Williams asked, momentarily taken aback. "No, Walter is completely different, another case entirely. And Mr. Woods is, well, he's adjusting, he's happy, but you don't need to be that way, it will work this time, you just have to do the exercises."

He followed her out the door. She paused, trying to remember her way back to the room that had the clothes she would need. Getting her bearings, she set out walking quickly down the corridor, the doctor following behind. She passed the busy waiting areas, and dodged the occasional nurse or orderly pushing a cart, the doctor taking long strides to keep up.

"You can't keep me here," Sarah said, staying ahead of him as he tried to come abreast of her.

"No, I can't," he said. "You came in voluntarily, and you can leave at any time. But you aren't yourself. If you do the exercises, you'll get it all back, all of it."

"All of what?" she shouted angrily, startling a man in the corridor as he dodged around him and continued walking briskly away from the doctor. "What did you take away from me? My mother? Why can't I remember my mother?"

"Because she was someone else's mother," Williams said, breathing heavily. "Cordelia and Theresa couldn't remember having a mother either. That's what all of this is for. To get all that back, to integrate. Please slow down, I'll take you anywhere you want to go, you can go anywhere you like, just please slow down so we can talk."

They had reached the elevator. Sarah pushed the button to go up, and after a few seconds, the door opened. They got in together. Sarah studied the buttons.

"Seventh floor," Williams said. "If we're going back to the recovery suite."

Sarah pressed the button marked seven.

"I'm leaving," she said. "Don't try to stop me."

"OK," Williams said. "I can't stop you anyway. But please listen to what I'm saying. Cordelia knows what the exercises are. You need to access her memories. Everyone's memories. There's a folder in your room, it has all the information in it, please take it with you. It has the exercises. You don't want to end up like Woods, really you don't."

"You just said he was happy," Sarah snapped, as the doors opened.

"A dog is happy," Williams said. "Blissfully ignorant. That's not what you want, trust me."

"I've been told you're the last person I should trust," Sarah said.

"Who said that?" Williams asked, following her quick strides again. "It doesn't matter, trust yourself. Trust Cordelia. Read the letter in the folder."

She found the door to her room, and jerked it open. She strode into the bedroom, and whipped off the robe. "A little privacy, please," she said, closing the bedroom door in the doctor's face as he started to enter.

A Distant Beacon

"Can you tell me where you're going?" the doctor said through the door.

"Home," Sarah said.

"Which one?" Williams asked.

"What the fuck does *that* mean?" Sarah called back. "Home."

She came out dressed in the clothes she had worn the day before. They were clean and put back where she had originally found them. Williams was standing in the middle of the room, holding a leather-bound notebook and a fashionable purse. He handed both to her.

"Please call me when you settle down," he said. "I can explain everything. But you have to start the exercises. Please, don't let too much time go before you start."

"Can you call me a cab?" Sarah asked.

"Your driver is staying at the motel across the street," Williams said. "Just call him." He pointed at her purse.

She opened it. It contained makeup, a phone, a small tablet computer, a set of keys, and a woman's wallet, among other things like tissues and a pen. "My driver," she said, staring at Williams as if he were speaking gibberish. She picked up the phone. "What's his number?"

The phone came to life. "Dialing," it said.

"What the fuck?" Sarah said, peering at the device in her hand.

"Hello?" it said, and a face appeared on the screen. "Oh, hi Mrs. Bellingham! Good to see you're up and around. You want me to pick you up something?"

"I'm going home," she said.

"Oh, that's great! They said it would be a couple weeks at least. Can you walk? Or should I bring a van?" The face looked up at her as a puppy would.

"I can walk," she said, glancing up at Williams. "Where should I say we'll meet?"

"The east lobby," Williams said to the phone.

"Give me ten minutes, tops," the man in the phone said, and the screen went dark.

Williams continued to plead with her as he led her down to the empty lobby of the Bellingham Wing. He had given up trying to get her to stay, but continued to stress the importance of doing the exercises outlined in the leather-bound notebook.

Outside the lobby, a tall man in a suit met them at the door, and led them to a long black car with tinted windows. Sarah recognized the man's face from the picture on the phone. Williams said nothing as she got into the car. He had said all he could say. The driver opened the rear door for Sarah to get in.

"5480 Shemara Street," Sarah told the driver when he had seated himself. She looked around the big car. There was a computer monitor and keyboard built into the back of the front passenger seat, and a rack of glasses above what must have been a small refrigerator.

"Changed your mind?" the driver said. "Shemara, I'll have to look that one up." He busied himself at the navigation console for several seconds. "It isn't coming up," he said. "What city?"

"Carpinteria," Sarah said.

A Distant Beacon

"Oh, that explains it. Long drive. You want music, or the news?"

"Actually," she said wearily, "if you don't mind, I think I'll lie down for a bit and rest."

"Of course," he said. He pulled away, and Sarah watched as the figure of Williams grew smaller through the back window. The car was wide, and she could almost stretch out on the leather seat.

Now, I have my life back. I'm in control.

She didn't remember falling asleep, but she woke as soon as the car stopped moving.

"I'll be right here," the driver said. "How long do you think you'll be?"

"You can go home," Sarah said, gazing out the window at her house. Something nagged at her, something was wrong with the trees, but she shrugged it off. She was tired, and wanted nothing more than to take a hot shower and fall into bed.

"You sure?" the driver asked, puzzled.

"I'll be fine," Sarah said. The driver made a small salute, and nodded. But he didn't leave. He watched her walk up to the porch.

None of the keys in the purse looked familiar. She fingered them one by one, searching for her house key. Finally, she gave up and reached down for the fake stone under the ferns beside the porch, and got out the spare key. She opened the door and walked in.

The carpet had been recently vacuumed, and there were two large bins of mail beside the door. Both of these observations puzzled her, but she walked into the bedroom, threw the purse and notebook onto the bed, and then walked into the bathroom to start the shower. She threw her clothes on the floor, and spent a long time in the shower, washing her hair twice, carefully fingering the sutured puckers behind her ears.

Drying off, she lay down on the bed, on top of the covers, but she wasn't sleepy. The nap in the car had apparently been enough.

The notebook was key to making sure she did not forget who she was, and to remembering what had happened during her missing periods. The dread she felt about what she had done during those periods was something she could feel in her chest. Something that made it hard to breathe. Maybe it was better not to know. *A dog is happy.*

But not knowing scared her as well. How could she protect herself if she didn't have all the information? More than that, she was just plain curious. What had been happening to her all her life in those dark empty times?

She opened the notebook, and began to read.

~

A Distant Beacon

David Archer's hangover was getting on Reynolds' nerves.

"So she heard the cops were coming and suddenly took off?" Archer grated irritatingly.

Alice Watkins was taking none of it. "That's what I would do, and I just met you."

"So anybody can just walk out of the looney bin these days?" he pressed on, not noticing her tone, and probably not even registering her words.

"We are a specialized treatment center, not a prison," Alice said. "We don't house dangerous patients, and we don't house anyone against their will. If you're feeling like you need something like that, you can try Salinas Valley."

Again, the taunt went over Archer's head. Reynolds was beginning to like Alice, despite his earlier interview.

"Did she say where she was going?" Reynolds asked politely.

"Home," Alice said. "Her driver picked her up in a limo."

"Did you witness that?" Archer said, pinching the bridge of his nose and closing his eyes.

"I heard it from Doctor Williams," Alice said. "He was upset. His major source of funding just walked out the door in a tiff."

Reynolds frowned. "So she was a donor, not a patient?"

"She was both. But that's about all I can say without seeing a court order." Alice seemed to like being able to say that.

"Medical issues aside," Reynolds said, "Did she talk to you at all about her husband's whereabouts?"

"I don't think so," Alice said.

"Even in her sleep?" Reynolds pushed.

"Well, about that I wouldn't know. If I saw her when she was asleep, she was sedated." Alice thought the question was strange.

"So she was sedated," Archer said, pointing out the new information.

"I can't tell you that," Alice said.

"But you can tell us when she entered, and when she left," Reynolds pointed out.

"I can get you that information. She's in and out a lot, but this last time was from last Monday morning to just a couple hours ago. She was supposed to be here another few weeks, at least."

"So," Archer said, "She checked in just after her husband checked out."

"Her husband was never here," Alice said.

"He meant figuratively," Reynolds said.

"He's dead?" Alice said, her hand to her mouth. "I just thought he was missing. You guys are from homicide, oh my god."

"He was just missing until some idiot talked too much back at the station," Reynolds said.

"Someone said he was dead?" Alice asked.

"That's all we can say without seeing a court order," Archer echoed.

"Oh my god, poor Cordelia, she must have heard," Alice said. "That explains it. She knows how important the exercises are."

A Distant Beacon

"She has contacts in the department?" Reynolds asked.

"I wouldn't know," Alice said. "But she's friends with the mayor. A campaign contributor."

"Damn," Archer said. "No wonder she's a step ahead of us."

"We'll need anything we can get on the limo and the driver," Reynolds said, mostly to Archer, but partly to Alice.

"Real nice guy," Alice said. "I forget his name, but he comes in every day to check on her, even when she's under. He'll be in the sign-in file."

"Any chance you got the license plate on the limo?" Reynolds asked.

Alice smiled. "Come on, detective. She's Cordelia Bellingham. The limo plate just says TYGAARD."

"Like her husband's company," Reynolds said, nodding. "Nothing after that, like a number?"

"Just the letters."

"Must be the husband's limo," Archer said.

Walter Hastings walked into the hallway. He had on a new tie, and he had unbuttoned the white lab coat to show it off.

"That should be all we need," Reynolds said, pulling out a business card and handing it to Alice. "Give me a call if you think of anything that might help." He turned to Walter, and Alice took the opportunity to leave as quickly as she could without actually running away.

"I told you it would come across your desk," Walter said, walking up to Reynolds.

"She's not the only one who talks too much," Reynolds said, looking over at Archer.

"You the guy who knows the perp?" Archer asked.

"You mean Cordelia," Walter said. "But she won't be going by that name now. Or any of the names she's used in the past."

"She has aliases?" Archer asked.

"Several. But that won't help you," Walter said. "I spoke with her. She's changed the way she dresses, and she'll be using a new name. I didn't ask her what the new name is, which is too bad, because now that she's left, I have no way to contact her."

"She's wearing a disguise?" Archer asked.

"It's subtle. The best ones are. You'd never know it was Cordelia; she walks differently, talks differently, and has different taste in clothes. It's too bad she left though, she's likely to kill off Theresa and Morganna if she doesn't stick to her treatment schedule."

"You're saying she's homicidal?" Reynolds asked.

"Not my words," Walter said. "But those two are goners if she doesn't get her head back together. It's happened before."

"To whom?" Reynolds asked.

"Woods," Walter said. "I don't know his first name. Poor guy. It's going to happen like that all over again, if she isn't in the program anymore. Nasty business."

"She confessed to you?" Reynolds asked.

"Oh, yes, often. It's therapeutic. While we do crossword puzzles together. She's very good, very smart, always one step ahead."

A Distant Beacon

"Like today," Archer said, looking at Reynolds.

Reynolds handed Walter his business card. "We have some checking to do," he said. "Give me a call if you remember anything more that might help."

"I'll do that," Walter said, smiling. He looked from Archer to Reynolds, and then to George the alpaca, who did not seem pleased, then back to Reynolds.

The two detectives left and Walter turned to George. "What?" he asked.

"Nothing," George said. "Too late now."

~

The next morning, Sarah looked down at the two large bins of mail by the door. She picked up a letter at random, a bill from the phone company, and opened it. It was just a normal bill. Why there would be so much mail was a puzzle. She started digging through the mail, searching for anything that wasn't a bill or some other routine item. She found nothing exceptional.

"Oh shit," she said, glancing again at that first phone bill. She stared at the date, not wanting to believe it.

This time it was seven years.

She began to weep softly. It wasn't fair. Seven years of her life, just gone.

"Shit!" she said, wiping the tears away, and digging through the bins. She sorted the bills into piles. There were no advertisements, no personal letters, just bills from the phone company, bank statements, the water bill, the gardening service, and the housekeeping service.

She stopped, studying the last bill in her hand. All the bills had been paid. She opened a bank statement. It showed automatic payments for phone, water, power, garbage, cleaning, everything. Her financial life was on autopilot.

She looked at the deposits. Every month, someone deposited $12,203.14 into her bank account. But it wasn't from any waitressing job, that was for sure. The payments were coming from a law firm.

She didn't remember ever working for a law firm. What kind of legal job makes that kind of money?

The balance on the account was larger than any waitress would have in her bank account. After the bills were paid, there had been

A Distant Beacon

almost ten thousand dollars left over. She looked at the bill — it was six years old.

She collected all of the bank statements, searching for the most recent. She opened it. Seven years of accumulation, at ten thousand a month. She had nearly a million dollars in her checking account.

No wonder the nurse had envied her health plan. She was loaded.

Why don't I know this shit?

She remembered the leather-bound notebook she had fallen asleep reading the night before. She got up and retrieved it, and started reading again. The exercises were supposed to help her find her memories, and keep the ones she had. It was time to start paying attention to the damned doctor's advice.

First exercise — write down as many of your favorite things as you can remember.

Second exercise — find as many familiar things as you can in your surroundings, and write down where you first encountered them.

Third exercise — make a list of all the dates that are important to you, such as birthdays, special holidays, anniversaries, and write down what you were doing on those days.

Fourth exercise— identify missing periods in your life, periods you can't remember, and try to find any information you can about what you were doing during those periods. Contact people you know who might be able to help, public records, saved emails, letters, mementos, whatever you can find.

There were dozens more exercises, but they all had the same basic idea. She was supposed to construct her own biography, in as much detail as she could.

"Well," she said out loud, "That's something I was about to do anyway."

Favorite things. She looked for her guitar, and found it in the bedroom closet. She'd never have put it there; it was always at hand, usually resting against the couch. She started to play, but it hurt her fingers. As if she had not played guitar in seven years.

That's ridiculous. Of course, I must have played the guitar. I always play the guitar.

She started to play again. The music came, but the muscles rebelled, especially on chords that required extra pressure. She continued playing, until her hands cramped up.

She put down the guitar and stood up, shaking her hands as she walked. She pulled open drawers in the desk, searching for her journal. She found it in the third drawer, a place she would never have put it.

If it had actually been a real journal, with dates and activities, it would have made some of the exercises much easier. But what she put in her journal were song lyrics she had composed. The songs came back to her as she read, and she got a pen and started writing notes in the margins, recalling what events or thoughts had caused her to write those songs. Some were easy, for others she had no idea when she had written them, or why.

When she could think of no more to add, she got up and carried the journal around the house, checking cupboards and closets, noting down any memories of when she had acquired any of the contents, or if they had any special meaning.

The painting in the living room stopped her in her tracks.

It was a picture of a lighthouse, as seen from the sea. Rocky cliffs were behind it as it stood alone on a low point of land, protected

A Distant Beacon

from the sea by walls of broken stone. It looked cold, the clouds hiding the sun, the waves crashing against the rocks.

The painting was signed *Morganna*. It meant something very important, but she had no idea what it might be. And she could not stop staring at the painting.

The nut job at the hospital had mentioned that name. It was a strange name, like something out of an old book, not a name a proud parent would give a little girl, not in this day and age.

She opened the journal to record her thoughts about the painting, and the name. She wrote down Morganna Wilson, and had no idea where the last name had come from. She must have known the artist when she bought the painting. She could not remember buying the painting.

> *I know I'm home when weary eyes first sight,*
> *The distant beacon of the Tygaard light.*

The poem came into her head, and she wrote down the first stanza in the journal. It wasn't a song. It was a poem, but it came to her the same way the song lyrics did. She tried to remember the rest of the poem, or anything about where she might have heard it or read it, but nothing came.
She looked at the painting again, and was certain she was seeing the Tygaard lighthouse, wherever that might be. It was very important. She just had no idea why.

Her examination and documentation of all the items in the house brought her back to the bedroom, where the clothes and purse from last night were lying on the floor by the nightstand. She picked up the purse and dumped its contents out onto the bed.

The makeup items were unusual. High-end cosmetics, in shades she would never have picked for herself. None of them seemed important, or came with any memories or emotions. The exercises were very keen on emotions, and she had to follow up and explore anything that brought an emotional response.

She picked up the phone. Another high-end device, and seven years newer than anything she remembered ever using. However, if she didn't think about how to use it, but just let her fingers play with it, the right things just happened. She was looking at a list of contacts. When she touched one, a face appeared on the screen, a snapshot of the person, probably taken with the same phone.

She scanned the names. They were in alphabetical order, and seemed to have no special importance. At least those in the A's. There were an enormous number of people in this woman's contact list.

She brought up the list of recent calls, and here the names and faces started to make sense. There was Williams, the doctor, and the face of the driver. She smiled. She'd been thinking of him as James, as in "Home, James," something you said to a limo driver. But his name was Peter Thompson, an unremarkable name, and one that brought up no special feelings, although the young man was good looking.

She opened the journal and wrote down the names and times of each call in the list. There were a lot of calls.

Cordelia Bellingham had figured out something Sarah never had. The blackouts weren't just missing days, lost memories. They were other personalities taking over. Cordelia had found a way to communicate with one of them, and had gone to great lengths to prevent it from happening again. However, she hadn't counted on Sarah being the one to wake up from whatever she had done to her head. *And I'll be damned if I let her take over, now that I'm in control.*

A Distant Beacon

Sarah picked up the tablet computer. It came to life in her hands, and presented a screen that expected a user name and password. Sarah tried several times to guess what the magic words were, but had no luck. She tried thinking about nothing at all, and letting her fingers do whatever they would do with the tablet, but nothing happened. She gave up and put down the tablet.

It was time to find out more about Cordelia Bellingham.

She put the journal and the exercise notebook into her guitar case, and took them out to the garage. Her little car was there, right where she had left it. Seven years' worth of dust covered it. Apparently, the cleaning service didn't cover the garage. The car was not plugged in.

All four tires were flat, but she was sure the pressure regulating system would fill them once she started the car. She opened the door, and caked dust fell from the car all around her, making her cough. Inside the car, it was clean, and she got in and sat down. The car did not awake.

She got out and found the cable, and wiped clean the charging port before she plugged the cable in. No lights came on in the car. The battery was so drained that it could not recognize the charging cable's negotiating protocol. She wasn't going anywhere in this car today.

She brushed dust from her clothes and went back inside. If she was going to Cordelia's house, it made more sense to use Cordelia's car anyway.

She scooped up all of Cordelia's things and put them back in the purse, except for the phone. She held that in her hand, and brought up the picture of the limo driver. She made the call.

It answered on the first ring. "Give me five minutes," the driver said, his face looking concerned. "In the meantime, take the battery out of the phone. They're probably tracking it even without the court order."

The picture went away, and Sarah glanced at the phone for a moment before turning it over and figuring out how to remove the battery. She put the phone and the battery back into the purse, and carried the purse and her guitar out to the front of the house, where she could watch the street from her window.

It was no more than a minute or two before a small gray sedan pulled to the curb, and the limo driver got out and started walking quickly up to the house. Sarah walked out of the door to meet him, pulling it shut clumsily behind her as she managed the guitar case.

The driver took the guitar case and quickly stowed it in the back seat, then opened the front passenger door for Sarah. She got in.

"Judge Ramsay called the house," he said. "He's stalling the police, but he can't for very long. They asked for a court order to search the grounds. Jameson said to get you, and keep you safe, and then he'll let them search. We can go back in when they're gone, but there are police watching all of Brookside, so we'll have to get in through the back."

"What are they looking for?" Sarah asked.

"You," Thompson said. "They think you killed your husband. Someone leaked it to the news about an hour ago. I brought some things from the house you can wear to keep from being recognized, but I think it's best to find a friendly spot to hole up for a couple hours."

"Shouldn't we just go to the police?" Sarah asked. She knew deep inside that she couldn't do that. Somehow, she was sure that

A Distant Beacon

Cordelia Bellingham had killed her husband. *Mr. Hyde went to sleep and Dr. Jekyll woke up.*

"Rule number one: nothing gets in the way of recovery. If someone is dying, your exercises come first. I made you that promise — we all did. And you can't do the recovery in jail."

He paused, and she watched his face as he tried to figure out how to say something.

"Yes?" she prompted.

"The doctor said you might not remember things that happened before you went under. He, um, he said you might have actually killed him." Peter Thompson kept his eyes fixed on the road ahead, his hands tight on the steering wheel.

"What do you think?" Sarah asked him.

"No way," he said. "I never met him, but I know you. You'd find a better way out than killing someone. You'd never do anything stupid, or without careful, thorough planning. Killing Wilson Bellingham right before going under anesthesia, that's not you. You're always in control."

She sounds like a real bitch.

"I know one other thing though," he said, lowering his voice. "If you did kill him, you'd get away with it." He turned to her and smiled, as if he were proud of her.

Shit. I need to know more about this woman.

There was an awkward silence for the next few miles. Sarah broke it by bringing up the exercises.

"So, one of my exercises is to ask people things about me. I don't think they mean whether or not I could get away with murder.

Stuff like, what are my favorite things, how did we first meet, what's the most emotional thing you remember me doing, stuff like that. So, fire away. Tell me about me."

"Most emotional," he started, and then stopped. "We first met four years ago. I had just passed all those driving tests your guys made us all do, and there were five of us who made the cut. You asked me what I would have done if I was driving Princess Diana and the paparazzos were chasing us."

He stopped, and she coaxed him on. "And you said?"

"I said I'd slow down, drive carefully, and shoot their cameras with a paintball gun. I had just driven a hundred and twenty miles an hour in a limo dodging every single traffic cone perfectly, and I just could not see doing that with the boss in the car."

"And what was the response?" she asked.

"You said don't point a gun at something I don't intend to kill. I learned the next morning I got the job." He turned off the freeway.

Did I shoot my husband?

"Favorite things," he said, pulling into a quiet street in a business district. "You like ice cream with gooey things and nuts. You like watching kids feed the ducks in the pond at the park. You like takeoffs and landings. You like old noisy cars that go really fast. With manual transmissions."

"Emotional moments," she prompted.

"You really want to go there?" Thompson asked.

"It's therapy," Sarah said.

He hesitated. "That time at the pool," he said.

A Distant Beacon

"Yes?"

"You were crying. It was late, almost midnight, and I was cutting across the patio from the garage to the main house. All the lights were out, and I couldn't tell it was you until I heard you crying." He turned his head to look at her.

"And then?"

"And then I took your hand and you hugged me, still crying. You were wet, and I held you. Then we both realized you weren't wearing a bathing suit, and you pushed away and walked back into the house. But you said 'thank you' before you went through the door."

"What was all the crying about?" Sarah asked, after a moment.

"I never knew. We never talked about it again."

Sarah felt sad about that, and recalled the warnings in the leather-bound notebook. In her current state, she was very receptive, her brain was plastic, and she would form strong relationships quickly, without the benefit of an inner skeptic that could hold her back. Thompson had opened up to her, and she felt a strong need to comfort him.

He pulled the car into a driveway, and rolled down the window to enter a code on a keypad. A garage door opened, and he drove the car inside.

"We're here," Thompson said.

"And where is here?" Sarah asked.

"Who knows," Thompson said. "But you own it, at least until escrow closes. Some piece of commercial real estate Jameson found on the books. No one will be looking here."

Sarah retrieved the guitar case from the back seat, and they entered the building proper. The ground floor was an empty carpeted expanse, with windows opening into a landscaped garden with a small waterfall and stream. She opened a glass door and stepped out into the enclosed garden, and found a seat on a bench. Thompson sat on the bench across from her.

"Time to write all that down," she said, opening the guitar case and pulling out the notebook.

"Fast cars that make noise," she said, scratching into the journal with a ballpoint pen. "Stick shift. Gooey ice cream."

"With nuts," Thompson said. "Or at least something crunchy, like toffee bits."

"Ducks in the park, paintball gun, the fun parts of plane trips," she said, writing quickly. "And crying by the pool naked."

She looked up at Thompson, who was not meeting her eyes. "Do I cry a lot?" she asked.

"Just that once," he said.

"Do I skinny dip a lot?"

"That I wouldn't know, ma'am," he said, smiling.

"But you checked the next night, just to see," she said, teasing.

"You were in Boston the next night," he said.

She wrote that down in the journal. Then she took the guitar out of the case, and held it, testing the tuning.

"I didn't know you played," Thompson said.

A Distant Beacon

"You drive me around everywhere, and you've never seen my guitar? Where I go, the guitar goes."

"Never," he said.

She began to play. Her fingertips were sore, and the muscles in her fingers were still not up to handling some of the chords that needed more pressure, so she altered the melody to make it easier to play.

"You're very good," Thompson said when she had finished.

"I didn't feel up to doing the vocals," she said. "I wrote that on the cliffs, watching the sun set. It was a Saturday night. There was a bonfire on the beach down below, and a guy, Donny something. He kept trying to convince me I should vote."

She put the guitar back in its case and picked up the journal again. "I'm supposed to write it down when I think of things like that," she said. "What year was that? Not a year when you voted for president. He was voting for some lady senator."

She wrote in the journal. "It's called *'If I should fall'*. The song I mean. A double entendre, so you don't know if the singer means fall in love or off the cliff. Whatever happened to Donny?"

She wrote the name in the journal.

"Emotional," she said, sanding her fingertips on the concrete below the bench. Build up the calluses again. Shit, seven *years*.

"How about a first kiss?" Thompson said.

"OK, but no tongue," she said, and they both laughed.

"Do you remember yours?" she asked him.

He thought for a while, and shook his head.

"I remember my first French kiss," she said. "I was pretending I knew everything, and had all kinds of experience, and I had heard about French kissing, and the kid I was dating said he'd never done it. So I kissed him, and stuck my tongue in his mouth and he swallowed his gum."

She wrote that down. "No dates though," she said. "I have the memories, but no idea what year it was. I'm supposed to make a timeline."

Thompson thought about that. "You could just put them in order," he said. "Then if you get a date for one, you can home in on the others. Or you could try to remember what grade you were in at school, or whether you had braces on, or acne."

"I had tits," Sarah said. "But no lipstick or eye shadow. That should narrow it down a bit."

"Not much more than 'first French kiss' did," Thompson said.

She put the pen down. "Shit!" she said. "I can't remember prom night, or losing my virginity, or my first period. How can someone remember a guy choking on his gum but not the first time she had sex?"

"Isn't that what this is all about?" Thompson asked. "The doctor said the exercises were to help you remember."

"He said that to you?"

"Actually, he said they were so you wouldn't forget. But that's kind of the same thing, isn't it?"

Sarah wasn't listening. She was looking at the name printed on the glass door.

"Tygaard Securities," she said.

A Distant Beacon

Thompson looked over at her, and then at the door. "I told you, this is one of your buildings," he said.

"Tell me about Tygaard," she said.

"Well, let's see, there's Tygaard Holdings, Tygaard Investments, Tygaard Securities, there's a bunch of them. Mr. Bellingham just about named everything Tygaard something."

"Tell me about Mr. Bellingham," she said.

"What do you want to know?" he asked.

"Whatever you know," she said, "just talk."

"Well, he's an investor. People give him their money, and he makes more of it, and takes a piece. He's one of the best there are, very successful. Built a huge business in just a few years, using his wife's money to start," he said, pointing at Sarah.

"Where did she get the money?" Sarah asked.

"No clue," he said. "Family money, probably, she always had that feeling about her, like she was from old money." He felt uncomfortable talking about her in the third person.

"What does he look like?"

"Bellingham? I have no clue. You're the only one I know who has ever seen him. He does everything in writing, never meets anyone in person; he's a germophobe and a recluse. I've never even seen a photo of him."

"You don't drive him around?" Sarah asked.

"No," he said. "And I don't know how he does it. He writes about conferences he's been to in Europe and Asia and South America, writes about the two of you in a hotel in Boston, but I always take you to the airport alone."

He studied her face. "You really don't remember, do you?" he said. "Do you think you could have done it, and forgot?"

"You mean kill him?" she asked.

He looked at the ground between them.

"I really don't know," she said. "I'd like to think I'm not that kind of person." *But Cordelia is.*

"Maybe he did something," Thompson said. "Maybe you were defending yourself."

She shrugged. "You'd think that would qualify as emotional, wouldn't you?" she said. "Maybe I'd remember if he had choked on his gum."

Thompson's phone buzzed in his pocket. He took it out and glanced at the screen.

"The police are gone," he said. "We can go back to the house."

Back. As if you'd been there before.

~

A Distant Beacon

Reynolds left the huge house and joined Archer on the flagstone driveway. The forensics team was loading their equipment into the trucks, but he already knew that the samples would tell them nothing in the lab. If there had been blood spilled in the house, the tech gear would have told them already.

"You notice any glaringly strange things about that house?" Reynolds asked Archer.

"Besides it being so big and full of expensive stuff?" Archer asked.

"I don't think he lives there," Reynolds said. "We went through every room. Did you see any sign of men's clothing in the closets? Any men's products in the bathrooms? Any reading material that wasn't on only one side of the bed?"

"Come to think of it, no," Archer said.

"If he doesn't live here, odds are he wasn't killed here," Reynolds said.

"So where does he live?" Archer asked.

"Everybody's playing dumb," Reynolds said. "They all claim they've never seen him. Like someone scripted it, told them all what to say. It's definitely a cover-up."

"So what's next?" Archer asked.

"I say we run a background check on everyone. Find something dirty about one of them, and put some pressure on, get them to spill something. And check Bellingham's credit cards and see where he buys stuff, or if he's got a favorite hotel or something." Reynolds looked back up at the big house.

Archer made a face. "Do you know how hard it was to get a warrant to search this place? Getting his credit card records is gonna be a real bitch."

Frank Carlisle joined the two detectives. "You said you wanted to see me," he said to Archer. He ignored Reynolds.

"Tell my friend here what you know about Mr. Woods," he said.

Carlisle was a short man, a head shorter than Reynolds was. He took a step back before looking up at the detective.

"That was a case came by my desk about a year ago. Landlord reported the guy missing, said he was late on the rent. But they were bowling buddies, and the guy also hadn't shown up for the league game. No known next of kin. So we checked with his employer." The man stopped and looked at Archer.

"Get this," Archer said, "It's good. The guy worked for Tygaard Investments, some kind of janitor or something."

"So we're following up, and guess what? The captain gets a phone call from Mrs. Wilson Bellingham herself. Says she moved the guy's job to Kansas City. Says he's doing fine there, no problem." Carlisle rocked back on his heels, his palms up.

"So, did you follow up, give the guy a phone call, and check his face against the file?" Reynolds asked.

"Hell no," Carlisle said. "The captain said close the file. It was Mrs. fucking Bellingham."

"So, your guy at the hospital is feeding us the straight dope," Archer said. "Looks like she offed the guy and got it covered up with just a phone call."

A Distant Beacon

"We'll see how long it stays covered up," Reynolds said. "The tech guys say Mrs. Bellingham hasn't been here in at least a week. All the sniffer gadgets come up zero, and the radar and thermal imaging isn't showing any hidden rooms or anyone hiding. We have video on the street, and patrols at both ends; if she comes back, we'll have her. But I don't think she's that stupid."

"She's got her own plane," Archer said. "If we flag her passport, we'll only know she's gone when she shows up in Costa Rica or something."

"Put someone watching the plane," Reynolds said.

"We don't have anybody left," Archer said.

Reynolds looked at Carlisle. "We have *him*," he said. He didn't sound happy about it.

~

Peter Thompson brought the car to a stop at a small ranch house on a quiet street with a view of the hill with the big house on one side, and the ocean on the other. He entered a code on his phone, and the garage door opened. He drove in.

"*Mi casa es su casa*," he said, waving his hands around the small garage. "Literally, I think. I mean you own the place, I just live here." He carried Sarah's guitar case in one hand and closed the car door with the other.

He opened the door that led to a small kitchen. "Excuse the mess; I don't get a lot of company." Some dishes were in the sink, some more on a small table in a breakfast nook. He led the way to the back door.

"It's a bit of a hike," he said, pointing up the hill to the big house. "But it's private. Trees on all sides blocking any view, and we can stay under the trees to avoid any drones or copters, but Jameson says it's clear anyway."

They walked along a dirt path under the trees, climbing the hill. It took them a while, but at the end of the path was an iron gate, with its lock open. Thompson replaced the lock when they had gone through.

Inside the tall rock walls, it was quiet. The sounds of the ocean and the sea birds didn't make it this far into the ornate garden. Ahead was the five-story-high wall of the house, dug into the hill for the most part, but all windows facing the ocean. A man in a blue suit came out of the house to meet them.

"Jameson," Thompson said, seeing her questioning look. "Head of security. Handles legal too. Good guy."

Michael Jameson had an athletic frame under the perfect-fitting suit, and he walked as she thought a fencer or an acrobat might

A Distant Beacon

walk. He was quick, and seemed to keep his weight on the balls of his feet more than the heels.

"Cordelia," he said, relieved to have her back where he could protect her. "They scoured the place, sent everyone home and used microwaves and terahertz scanners everywhere. They used sniffers and vacuumed everywhere; if we'd had a rat problem, they would have found them. I don't think they'll be back anytime soon, but you won't want to be here if they do."

Sarah scanned the room. The ceiling was at least thirty feet high, and Jameson's voice echoed off marble floors and granite walls. There were paintings and tapestries on the walls, including a giant woven forest scene, but they did little to deaden the sound.

"I don't intend to stay long," Sarah said. "But do you think it's OK to spend the night?"

"Definitely one night, probably even two," Jameson said. "We'll have half a day's warning of any court order."

"I'm only here because I need to do some exercises," she said. "Memory exercises, part of my therapy," she explained to Jameson.

"Doctor Williams filled us in," Jameson said. "He said you might not remember all the prep we did in the past weeks, but we're ready to help. I have all the stuff ready in the library, but we're supposed to tour the house. We talked about touring the grounds as well, but I don't think that's wise at this time."

Sarah followed him into the library, Thompson following behind with the guitar case.

In the library, there was a large oak table, completely covered with various objects. Jameson watched as she took in the room.

"You really don't remember, do you?" he asked.

She shook her head.

"Here is the catalog of items you set out," Jameson said, handing her a stapled stack of paper. "Items, dates, what each one means, why it is important. Does anything come back to you?"

She scanned at the list. African mask, gift from ambassador from Mali, killed in the coup two years later. Pen used to sign the worker's rights bill, cost us $80 million in lobbying and campaign donations to get passed. Meteorite collected by Cordelia Bellingham in Antarctica. Wedding band and engagement ring.

She looked down at her hands. There was no sign that she wore any rings for any length of time.

The table held many similar items, each something that should have held special meaning to Cordelia Bellingham, something she wanted not to ever forget. To Sarah, they meant nothing.

When she had handled the last item, a hand-carved flute from a trip to Bolivia, she handed the list to Thompson.

"This should go with the journal," she said, pointing to the guitar case. "It may mean something later. The book says the exercises will take time to work."

He took the papers and Sarah started walking through the huge house, visiting each room, examining each piece of furniture, looking out of each window. She stopped in a wide hallway with a large painting of a lighthouse on the far wall. She rushed up to read the signature: *Morganna*.

"This," she said to the two men. "This is special, this means something. What do you know about this painting? Where is that lighthouse?"

A Distant Beacon

The two men looked at one another. Neither knew anything about the painting. Jameson brought out his phone and dictated a note to find out everything about the painting of a lighthouse in the south hall.

"I think it's the Tygaard Light," she said. "It's important somehow."

I know I'm home... But this didn't feel like home.

~

The exercises weren't doing what they were supposed to do. As far as Sarah could tell, she hadn't lost any memories (but how would you know?). But she was also not regaining any memories from her dark periods. None of the special items from Cordelia Bellingham's life had any meaning for Sarah, and none of them brought back any images or feelings.

The others had left, and Sarah was alone, at least on this floor of the house. She sat on the big bed, her back against the headboard, cushioned by a mountain of expensive pillows, the leather-bound exercise notebook open in her lap. There had to be more she could be doing.

She had her memories. She had this house, with all of Cordelia's memories locked inaccessibly in objects lying on a table. Objects were not enough. She was getting fleeting feelings of a past connection when she spoke with Peter Thompson, but there had been little emotional attachment between Peter and Cordelia. Likewise with Jameson — she had grilled him according to the notebook, as she had Thompson, but nothing had quite clicked. Just some vague sense of the familiar.

People were clearly better than objects, but she would need people that she had an emotional relationship with. Someone she loved, someone she hated, someone she feared.

Oh, shit. Atlanta.

The feeling she had in the back of her spine told her that she was on the right track. The thought of going back to Atlanta terrified her. That was good, right? Emotion! It was what was missing. Cordelia Bellingham seemed to have arranged her life to be free of emotional attachments. Everything was business, even the charities.

A Distant Beacon

No wonder even the closest people to her seemed to be certain she had killed her husband. Jameson acted as if he was protecting a battered wife from going away for murdering her tormentor. Did he know? Had he helped her kill him? Is that why he was so concerned that she didn't get caught?

Thompson claimed he thought she would never do something like that, not because it was wrong, but because it sounded stupid or unplanned. Those last two were not Cordelia Bellingham. But murderess could be, and he was sure she would get away with it.

Something or someone in Atlanta scared her, or at least filled her with this vague dread. It was as if she had done something terrible in Atlanta, and everyone there knew it.

She reached over the side of the bed to pull the guitar into her lap. Her fingers still hurt when she played, but she didn't stop. The music didn't make the dread go away, but she could keep it at bay for a while, fingers pressing on strings, fingers plucking at strings. In her head, she heard piano music. She didn't play piano, but the music she coaxed from the guitar, she was sure, she had first heard on a piano. She could picture fingers on the keys.

When her fingers could take no more, she put the guitar down by the side of the bed again, and struggled under the covers. The sheets had been pulled tight, as if she were in a hotel bed. She threw all but one of the pillows off the bed, and squeezed that one around her ears after turning out the light. The world still wouldn't go away, and Atlanta was still there, waiting for her.

~

"Your travel kit," Jameson said the next morning, handing her a leather case. "I put a new SIM chip in your phone, and packed two pre-paid cash-only phones as well. Use those once, and throw them away afterwards. Call the South Africa office; they're less likely to trace that. They can get a message to me securely."

Sarah took the case, and opened it to look inside. The phones, the tablet computer she did not know how to access, a passport, and Cordelia's wallet all sat beside three leather pouches. She opened one. It was packed full of large denomination Euro notes. Another was U.S. currency, mostly hundreds, and the third was Japanese yen.

Jameson watched as she examined the money. "FedEx those to yourself if you leave the country," he said. "You don't want customs wondering about them."

A partition in the top of the case dropped down at her touch, revealing wrinkle-resistant clothes vacuum-sealed in clear plastic.

"I'm not leaving the country," she said.

"Don't say it," Jameson said. "We don't need to know where you are, and if we don't know, we can't accidentally reveal it."

"You think of everything," she said.

"I only wish." Jameson lifted another, much larger suitcase, and set it down next to the travel case. "Clothes and shoes," he said. "In case you're not up to shopping. The credit cards in your wallet are from Jill in Operations. Just in case. She travels a lot for the firm, and using them won't ring any alarms. And there is a company card as well, but using a Tygaard account should be a last resort."

Thompson took the two cases and left, presumably carrying them back to his house where the car was. Jameson waited until he was

A Distant Beacon

gone, and then said, "He'll be taking you to LAX. They are probably watching your jet, so we arranged for a charter to Denver. There's a convention there next week, and we'll be sending an advance team there, or so everyone has been told. You'll have the flight to yourself. The crew is discreet, it won't matter if they recognize you, but don't introduce yourself."

They walked together under the trees, down the hill to Peter Thompson's house. Walking through it to the garage, she noticed it looked scrubbed clean, as if for an open house. She smiled. Nothing in the big Bellingham house had said 'lived-in' like a stack of dishes in the sink. That house had mirrored its emotionless, efficient, business-like owner. She didn't say ruthless.

Chapter Four

She had asked the cab driver for the classiest hotel in Atlanta, something with charm, nothing cheap. She had handed him a one hundred dollar bill, and said 'Not your usual place.' He had brought her *here*.

The lobby reminded her of Cordelia Bellingham's house. Marble floors, high ceiling, wall hangings, but with acoustic tiles in the ceiling to cut down the reverberation.

She didn't immediately walk up to the desk, but wandered in the lobby as if meeting someone. She wanted to get a feel for the place before deciding to stay.

A grand piano took up one corner of the lobby, and she walked over to it. The sheet music was foreign to her, not the tablature she used for the guitar. It looked far more complicated than the simple vocal melodies she always ignored whenever she had used sheet music. She could only sight-read the chord patterns for the guitar; notes on a staff required counting lines and recalling *every good boy does fine*.

Her fingers idly pressed keys, and pleasant sounds came from inside the piano. She sat down on the bench and let her fingers wander softly among the keys as she surveyed the room. A couple with luggage walked up to the desk and checked in. A man in a business suit walked out of the elevator, and her brain said *Armani*. The Sarah part of her wondered if it were true, but the Cordelia part was sure of it.

She had begun noticing the Cordelia part of her in the charter plane. Cordelia knew where things were, knew what to expect. Sarah had never been on a chartered jet, alone in a huge space with a couch and reclining chairs, a desk to work at, and a big-screen television. Cordelia appreciated the vintage on the wine. Sarah drank none of it.

The exercise book had mentioned nothing about this. Sarah began to think that the whole idea of the notebook had been wishful thinking. No one had gone through this successfully before; the book was full of guesswork.

Finding situations where Cordelia would be at home, and Sarah wouldn't, and then letting her brain work on auto-pilot — that seemed to be the way to bridge the gap, to dredge up little bits of Cordelia to examine. The problem would be making sure Cordelia didn't take over. To lose what made her Sarah was the same thing as death. And this time she might not ever come back.

There had been no piano in Cordelia Bellingham's big house. Sarah was sure Cordelia didn't play. So whose fingers were making these nice sounds come out of the big concert grand? It was something about being in Atlanta.

In the mirrored wall, she kept part of her attention on the luggage she had left next to the large couch. The suitcase and travel kit had locks, but the purse did not. When she saw the young man sit next to them on the couch, she was ready to rise up and claim them, but he unfolded a newspaper and began to read. She watched him in the mirror, pretending to be absorbed in playing, but if she thought about what her fingers were doing, she was sure they would stumble. Of all the luggage, the only thing she really cared about was the beat-up guitar case.

She found that instead of being upset, shocked, angry, or even surprised when she saw his hand slip discreetly into her purse and remove her wallet she found she was only amused. It was like watching a television mystery. She was seeing someone robbed, right here in a classy hotel. Cordelia's wallet had no particular claim on Sarah's loyalty. *Serves you right, bitch.*

She continued to play, watching the back of the newspaper move more than it would have if someone had actually been reading it. Was he removing the large wad of cash in there? Taking the credit cards that she was not going to ever use, the ones that had Cordelia's name on them?

As she watched, the hand and the wallet slipped back into the purse, and the hand returned without the wallet. After about half a minute, the newspaper again folded, and the young man stood up. *Off-the-rack suit, doesn't match the shoes, hair not recently trimmed.* Cordelia saw the clothes. Sarah saw the man: intelligent eyes, nice face, no five-o'clock shadow, even now at something after 8 pm. Cocky, sure of himself. Quite pleased with something, perhaps the score he had just made out of Cordelia's wallet.

The piece ended, and Sarah recognized it as the piece she had played the night before, on the guitar. Those parts that had been tricky on the guitar had fallen naturally from her fingers on the keys. The cocky young man was by the door, as if he was waiting for someone. She walked over to retrieve her luggage and check in. This was definitely where she wanted to stay while she was in Atlanta.

At the desk, she didn't even bother with the purse or the wallet. She had placed Jill Waterston's credit card and California driver's license in her pocket during the cab ride, and she presented them to the desk clerk. The photo was close enough, and the clerk didn't even examine it anyway.

"Do you have a suite?" she asked. "Something with a view, perhaps? Something nice, I may be entertaining, if the senator agrees with our land-use proposal." She slid another hundred-dollar bill onto the counter towards his hand. It slid quietly off the counter without comment, into a pants pocket.

"We can certainly set you up," he said. "How long will you be staying?"

"I'm thinking a week at least," she said. "Taking in some scenery, doing a little negotiating. Sometimes it can take time."

"We have the Orchid suite," he said. "Twelve fifty a night," he added in a lower voice. "Will that be OK?"

"That will do nicely," Sarah said, letting Cordelia handle the tone.

As a porter was gathering her luggage, the young man with the newspaper approached her.

"Cordelia?" he said. "Wow, imagine meeting you here in Atlanta. I think the last time we met was on the west coast, Santa Barbara, I think. It's been a long time!"

Sarah smiled broadly. The other shoe had dropped. He was setting her up for a con. The Cordelia part of her brain saw this as entertainment. What fun! What a charming, clueless young con man. Cordelia was going to chew him up and spit him out, and have great fun doing it. Sarah began to feel sympathy for Cordelia's latest victim, but let Cordelia have a little bit more control, to see how she would handle this.

Still grinning, she took his proffered hand and shook it politely. "I'm afraid my brain is a little jet-lagged," she said. "I'm completely blanking on your name. From the government finance conference, what, two years ago?"

He took the bait immediately. "Yes! Douglas Warwick. I remember you well, you made quite an impression on everyone, or at least that's the way I remember it." He looked at the porter and the luggage. "Are you travelling alone? Here, take my card, and call me if you get some time. I'd love to buy you a drink and chat some more. I'm sure I could learn a lot from you again."

She took the card. "That would be lovely. Not this evening, I'm afraid, but perhaps tomorrow. I'm here for at least a week, so I'm in no rush."

"I'm down the street," he said, "but I have colleagues and customers staying here, so I'm in and out. We may run into one another."

I'm sure we will.

She followed the porter into the elevator, and tipped him well when he had set up her luggage in the suite.

When he had gone, she sank into the pillows on the bed and closed her eyes. She reexamined the things Cordelia had noticed in the lobby.

The young man was pretending to be in a class or two above his upbringing. His diction was practiced, but flawed, as if he had learned from watching television. The suit was noticeably more expensive than the shoes, a dead give-away to alert eyes.

The desk clerk had noticed the photo in the ID did not match the face, and would expect a large tip every evening.

Sarah had been watching the guitar case. Cordelia had been watching the con man. Who had been playing the piano?

She turned her attention to the piano playing. The piece meant something to the fingers playing it. There had been feeling there. She fished for the name of the piece, but came up with nothing. There was a personality associated with the music, that of someone she had an interest in. Probably a man. Someone she cared about.

That was all she could get. However, it showed she was on the right track. She had found an emotional moment that meant something to someone other than Sarah or Cordelia. The piano was the key to reaching that person.

The key to Cordelia was reading people. And business. And manipulating people. Cordelia was always in charge when someone needed to be in charge. She could manage people, and she could manage situations. She was imperturbable. She was never afraid of losing.

Sarah got out the guitar and began to play the melody again, this time working out the tricky bits and staying true to the original. Her fingers were getting the calluses back, and it was no longer so painful to play. Her finger strength was not yet completely recovered, but it was coming along. She fished for any words that might accompany the melody. If she had some words, she could look up the song, get the title, and maybe learn some more about who had been playing the piano.

But hey, I can play the piano. How cool is that?

~

The next morning, she rented a car. Her recollections of where she had awakened in Atlanta were unclear, and she drove around the city trying to find anything she remembered. The Buckhead area near the hotel was nothing like the tree-lined streets she remembered, with the big houses, where no one stopped for hitchhikers.

She drove west, and the landscape changed. This was more like it. Almost due north of downtown, the streets wound through low hills, and the trees blocked the view of anything further than a block or two.

She drove around the area for three hours without finding a single thing that sparked a memory.

She tried to picture the house as she had left it. It was large, perhaps seven or eight bedrooms. There was a huge circle of paving stones in the front, where vehicles could park or simply turn around and go back. There was a large pond.

Several things made her feel she was on the right track. All the streets seemed to end in 'northwest', no matter which direction the street went. She remembered making fun of the pretentious name, but no amount of coaxing could bring the name to the top of her consciousness.

And these are MY memories, not Cordelia's. Sheesh!

This was Cordelia's type of place, and her comments bubbled to the top whenever an expensive car approached, or a house showed a particularly awful display of bad taste and conspicuous extravagance. Where the Bellingham estate had been a quiet museum where old money would feel at home, this area was in-your-face display designed to prove to high school bullies that the owners had moved up in the world, way, way up.

A Distant Beacon

She kept driving. She was sure that she was in the right area, or only a few miles away. Just around the corner, perhaps. Maybe that street a few blocks back, maybe that would have brought her there. It was easy to get caught up in the random wandering search. She finally called it quits. She was not going to stumble on it. She needed a search plan, a method, and maybe some help.

She drove back to Buckhead, pulling out the business card from her purse (no longer *'Cordelia's purse'*, she noted). A local might help the search. Someone who knew the area, and someone who would be eager to explore an area filled with high value targets.

Cordelia didn't want to meet the young man in a rental car. Sarah relaxed, and let Cordelia find the library, where she sent an email to Jameson, directing him to find a high-end sports car somewhere in Atlanta, something like a an Aston Martin or a Lamborghini, nothing brand new or electric, but flashy and noisy. Buy it and have it waiting for anyone presenting a Tygaard Securities credit card. She'd wait for a reply. Don't be long.

While she waited, Sarah brought up real estate listings for the area north of Atlanta. She entered the type of home she was looking for. Five bedrooms or more. Acreage. Price? Cordelia felt nothing less than five million would do.

She examined the photos that came up in response. She hadn't expected the house to be for sale, and it wasn't. But the houses she saw fit with her recollection of the type of house it had been.

One address stood out. Tuxedo Park. That was the pretentious name she had made fun of.

The email reply came back. *Lamborghini Gallardo, low miles.* An address followed. The map showed it to the north, on the way to Roswell. It did not take long to get there.

Cordelia handled the salesman, showing him the Tygaard card, and asking to see the Gallardo. She handed him the keys to the rental car, and said politely "See that this gets back home, would you?" and took the keys to the Lamborghini. In all, the transaction took no more than seven or eight minutes.

Sarah ducked into the low driver's seat and found the controls to adjust it. Fearing she would damage her new quarter-million dollar car, she eased out of the lot and practiced driving the beast on quiet city streets before getting on the highway. However, Cordelia was at home in the car, and punched it as it quickly came up to speed. Very quickly.

She smiled at the parking valet when she got to the hotel, and handed him the keys and a large bill. "Keep it running for me dear," she said. "I won't be long."

She went to her room and changed into something Cordelia thought would impress the young con man, and called him from the room phone. He answered his cell phone on the second ring.

"Hi, it's Cordelia," she said causally. "I have a bit of an adventure planned for this afternoon, and a local guide would make it so much easier and more fun. I was wondering if you were free. I know it is very spur of the moment, but I could pick you up in a minute or two anywhere you like. It will be fun, I promise."

She started mentally counting, but had not gotten to three before he enthusiastically agreed to meet. He'd drop by the hotel; he was only a couple minutes' walk away. Cordelia had called it, Sarah thought. He'd drop whatever he was doing for the best mark he'd ever seen.

She met him at the lobby door, and the valet pulled up at exactly the right moment. She walked to the open driver's door and stopped, taking the keys from the valet and dangling them from a finger pointed at Douglas Warwick. "Unless you'd like to drive?" she asked coyly.

He glanced at the car, back at Sarah, and winked. "Maybe later," he said, and reached for the door. Sarah took the car out onto the road sedately, but opened it up on the highway, pressing them both back into the seats.

"Nice ride," Warwick said.

"Picked it up an hour ago," she said. "I remember when they used to need breaking in. Who wants that?" She overtook a car and then pulled back into the center lane, adjusting her speed to match the traffic.

"I'm looking for a house in the Tuxedo Park area," she said. "I am trying to remember exactly where, and I don't have an address. I'm sure I'll know it when I see it. Two story, blue slate roof, columns around the porch, one big gable in the center, next door to a much larger Mediterranean with a mission tile roof. I just can't remember which street it was, or who lived there."

"I may not be all that familiar with the neighborhood," Warwick said. "But I'll be happy to help you look."

"I'll just be happy for the company," Sarah said, giving his thigh a quick squeeze with her right hand. "It should be fun, a little adventure drive." Cordelia may have been manipulating the young man, but Sarah genuinely was happy for his company. She wondered which part of her was really in control. *Be more careful!*

Warwick seemed to be enjoying the ride, examining the car's interior and finding things that he liked. "So, what are you up to, business-wise these days?" he asked conversationally.

"Same as always," she said, "looking for companies that are in trouble, seeing if we have the people and connections to turn that around. Then we buy them, fix them, and merge them into the main business or sell them."

This seemed to remind him of something. "Hey, that sounds like you might be interested in this guy that's been sending me tips. I haven't bought anything, but he claims he has built some software that can analyze transactions in the penny stocks, and find companies that are about to double or more in value. I just ignored him for a while, he's an old college buddy, but he's been right on the money five times out of five."

She smiled. Cordelia was having fun with this.

"Five times in a row? Maybe you should pay more attention to him. We have software that tries that, looking at fundamentals, market externals, and that kind of thing, but it doesn't even get to forty percent accuracy." She took a turn a little fast, and the car seemed glued to the road, pushing both of them into the sides of the seats.

"I thought about it," he said. "But instead what I think I'll do is put some pretend money into a spreadsheet, and watch what happens after a few imaginary trades. He says I can turn a hundred K into a million in a couple weeks. If the spreadsheet says I'm a million up before the month is out, I'll buy in for real."

"Playing it safe," she said. "Let's do this. Make four entries in your spreadsheet. One for each of us, with a hundred each in your buddy's picks. And another one for each of us, with another hundred in our own picks. Then at the end of the month, we subtract our gains from his gains, and see who is the better investor, the two of us, or your friend."

He grinned. "I'll do that," he said. "And when you blow right past him, I'll let him know I'm putting my money on you."

A Distant Beacon

"We play a game like that in the office," she said. "The analyst with the best return after a month gets to name his favorite charity. The others have to donate the difference between his score and theirs."

"I'll bet you win every time," he said.

"Just the opposite, actually. I haven't won once. I'm just the boss; these guys are the real analysts. But it's all in good fun, and we can all use the deductions come April." She grinned at him, and turned another fast corner.

They had come to Tuxedo Park, and she slowed down to scan the houses. "It's set back from the road," she said, "and the driveway becomes a circle when it gets to the house. The street had a name that made me laugh. It was incongruous or something, like naming a Great Dane 'Shorty'. I wish I could remember it."

She drove down the street, looking down each driveway. The trees made it hard to see unless you were right in front of the house.

"See that Mediterranean?" she pointed out. "There was a house like that next door, the red tile roof, the white stucco walls. The house was bigger than this one, maybe twice the size or better."

They drove past another five or six houses. "So, what's the deal with this house?" Warwick asked.

"Well," she said, hesitating. She didn't actually know the answer. "How about we say it's complicated, and leave it at that for the moment."

"Ah," he said. "I understand complicated. Say no more."

The afternoon passed by and none of the houses or streets struck Sarah as familiar. Finally, she was ready to stop for the day.

"Can I treat you to dinner?" she asked coyly. "I've enjoyed our talk, and I'm not sure I want the day to end just yet." Sarah was back in complete control, and she didn't want to be alone.

"I'd be delighted," he said.

"I've been told the Swan Coach House is nice," she said. "And it isn't far." She had scouted the restaurant earlier. Something quaint and historical, but not intimidating to the young con man.

After dinner, she brought him back to the hotel bar for drinks, but pleaded fatigue after only one, and offered to drive him back to his hotel. He declined politely, saying he wanted to walk off his dinner; it was such a nice night out. She had decided he lived somewhere nearby, and wasn't staying in one of the fancy hotels, and she did not press him.

Instead of returning to her room, she used the office space set aside for guests, and brought up maps of Tuxedo Park, studying each road name. In the ride with Warwick, she had remembered the name sounding odd or making her laugh. But it had been a bit embarrassing to recall, like the joke was in bad taste, or only she would think it was funny.

When she found it, she understood. The Sarah of ten years ago would have assumed that all the wealthy people in Tuxedo Park were white, and living on a street called Blackland was cause for amusement.

She had passed right by the street, and not gone down it. But tomorrow was another day.

Chapter Five

"I don't get it," Reynolds said to the clerk who had brought him the two folders. "Is Wilson Bellingham a person or a company?"

"Both," the man said, pointing to one folder. "There's a company started by Lee Wilson and Walter Bellingham. They did a lot of investing for people, mostly as a hedge fund. The Bellingham guy died, and there is a file number on that with a DEA tag, so there must have been some kind of investigation. We have a request in to the DEA for that file. The company died when the other partner washed up on the coast burned to a crisp with bullet holes in him."

"And this guy?" Reynolds asked, thumping his index finger down on the other folder.

"That's your mystery man. The dates overlap by about three years. He was also a hedge fund guy. The one everyone says is a genius at it. Never went into any of the popular stocks that all tanked in the big crash. Just steadily made money for everybody, and everybody wanted in but he wasn't taking new clients until about six years ago. That's when people started really hearing about him, the guy who was so germophobic and private that he never met anyone in person, and never even did video. No photos of the guy, it's like he bought up all his high school yearbooks and burned them."

David Archer leaned over to Reynolds so close that he could tell what brand of beer the man had for lunch. "You know what they say here in homicide," he said, looking up at the clerk. "There's no such thing as a coincidence."

Reynolds opened the folder. There were photocopies of business journal and newspaper articles, copies of public documents for companies he was on the board of, or had interests in. But the folder was thin. There was very little known about Wilson

Bellingham other than speculation and what was in public documents. He slid the folder over to Archer, and pulled out four different sheets of paper, spreading them out on the desk.

"You see anything funny about these?" he asked.

Archer examined the papers. Reynolds got impatient, and pointed at the four lines that had Bellingham's name on them.

"No salary, no stock, no options," Archer said, studying each page in turn. "The guy works for free," he said.

"I'd love to see his tax returns," Reynolds said.

"Um," the clerk began, reaching for the folder. "There's a mention of that," he said, rifling through the articles. "Here it is. It says he avoids conflicts of interest with his clients by keeping all his personal funds in tax-free municipal bonds. Here's the part I just loved. 'He keeps his life simple. On his income tax returns each year it simply says *no taxable income*.'"

"That must be nice," Archer said.

"Don't go getting jealous of a dead rich guy," Reynolds said. "He was so paranoid it made it easy for his wife to kill him. Her only problem was that when he stopped sending his emails, the world went ballistic. Otherwise, nobody would have even known he was dead."

Archer was scanning the articles, reading quickly with his finger following the lines of text.

"What," Reynolds asked, annoyed at the behavior.

"Just looking for any mention of places he hung out in," Archer said. "She didn't kill the guy in the house. He didn't even live there. So where did he live?"

Reynolds got out a much thicker folder, then another, and a third, and stacked them in front of Archer. "The Mrs. is a much more public figure," he said. "Instead of trying to find the guy who hides from his shadow, find out where the lady's been, and see if she visits him on any kind of regular basis."

"You're kidding me, right?" Archer said, looking at the four-inch high stack of paper.

Reynolds reached for the top folder, the thinnest of the three. "I'll take one. You take another. And here kid," he said, handing the last folder to the clerk. "How would you like to play detective?"

"Gee, thanks," he said sarcastically, taking the folder. He started to walk away.

"Not so fast," Reynolds said. "Pull up a chair; we'll keep it all in one room. When you see a place, write it down on this," he said, pulling a blank sheet from a pad. "But if it's already on the list, just add a tick mark. We'll sort by ticks when we're done, and start at the top."

"What about lunch?" the clerk asked.

Reynolds reached into his pocket and pulled out a dollar. "Buy yourself a Kit Kat," he said, pointing to the vending machine in the hallway.

~

The next morning Douglas Warwick surprised Sarah in the hotel lobby.

"They said they had no record of you staying here," he said.

She smiled and winked at him. "Some of us like our privacy," she said.

He was a little taken aback, but recovered quickly. "I didn't mean to be a pest," he said. "I just set up the spreadsheet for our little game, and wanted to get it to you. But I don't have an email address or a phone number for you."

She looked at him for a moment, thinking silently. "Open up a free email account somewhere, and tell me the password. We can use that to communicate. You won't even need to send the email; we can both just read the drafts."

"You really do like your privacy," he said.

"A habit one gets into after a while," she said. Sarah wondered what other habits Cordelia might have that would make it easier to get away with murder.

"I'll set that up then," he said. "I'll just leave the password with the desk clerk."

Then he realized he still didn't know who to leave it for. "But that won't work, will it?"

She hadn't planned to have company along when she got to the Tuxedo Park house, but as she considered it, she felt it might be safer to have someone with her. She could sense the fear of embarrassment part of her was feeling, but the Cordelia and Sarah parts were feeling no sympathy.

A Distant Beacon

"Come along," she said. "Same as yesterday, but this time I know what street we're looking for. You can play with your phone in the car and set up the email account."

By the time they reached Blackland Road, he had the account set up. He linked his phone to the big console display in the car so he could show her the details.

"He said Portland Chemical was set to at least double in the next five days," he said. "So I set us both up with 100k in that. And I tried to find something I thought might be a good bet for my pick, but I couldn't find anything I thought was going to jump like that. I figured for that kind of volatility, I'd need to go with options, so I bought some calls on West Texas Crude. Now I'm hoping something bad happens in the Middle East."

She turned onto Blackland Road, and pointed out the window. "This is the street. Look for a circle at the end of the driveway, or a tile roof, or porch columns."

The trees were higher than what she had expected. It had been almost eleven years, that should be no surprise.

"You could lose the entire 100k that way," she said. "Would you have done that if it were real money?"

"Tile roof," he said, pointing. She looked in that direction, and slowed the car to a crawl. Neither of the houses on either side seemed right.

"Mark the address," she said. "We'll come back if we don't find a porch with columns. Someone may have redecorated."

She drove on, still rather slowly.

"It's only 100k," he said. "And it goes to charity, right?"

"If you lose it, you lose it," she said. "Then you still owe the difference between us to charity."

"Ah, of course," he said. "But we're still talking play money here, right?"

She smiled broadly. "Let's see how you feel after a few rounds of play. If you want to play for real after three or four, you just say."

Her stomach tightened suddenly, and her foot slammed down hard on the brake. Warwick's shoulder belt dug into his chest as he heard her say, "Shit! This is it!"

They had only been travelling at a few miles per hour, but the sudden stop had still locked both seat belts momentarily. She backed the car up to look straight down the driveway. It ended in a circle, in front of a porch with a roof supported by four tall white columns. Ahead she could see the top of a red tile roof on the house next door.

She backed the car farther, and parked at the curb. She sat for a moment, staring at the house, her heart beating quickly in her chest. She took a deep breath, and let it out slowly.

"What now?" Warwick asked.

The part of her that wanted to run away almost took control. Cordelia's firm authority overcame it. "We knock on the door, and see who is home," she said.

It was a gated driveway, but the gates were wide open. Sarah locked the car behind them, and they walked up the long driveway to the circle. In the center was a fountain with no water in it. They walked around it and up the steps to the big double doors.

Each door had a large ornate brass knocker, but a more utilitarian doorbell with a lighted white plastic button was on the wall to the

A Distant Beacon

left of the doors. She pressed it, and heard chimes playing inside the house.

Ringing the bell was as far as her plans had gone. She had no idea what she would say when someone came to the door. Would the same maid that had been here ten years ago answer? Would she remember Sarah?

The door on the left opened, and a man stood in the doorway, looking first at Warwick, and then at Sarah.

Oh my god, it's Drake.

Memories of when she had last seen him began to flood in.

"Theresa?" the man said.

"Hi Drake," she said. "Long time."

He stood in the doorway, studying her. "You have a lot of nerve," he said.

She studied him back. His temples had started to gray, and his hair might have thinned, or receded a bit. But she had recognized him. She realized tears were falling down her cheeks, and was afraid her voice would crack if she spoke.

"Mother died hating you for what you did," he said. "We searched for you. The police just laughed at us. We hired private detectives. You just disappeared."

Theresa was about to rush to him and put her arms around him, and bury her face in his chest. Cordelia was having none of it, and, ignoring the tears, straightened her back and looked him in the eye. "Are you going to invite us in?" she said, every bit in control.

He looked from one of them to the other. Warwick avoided his gaze. "I think not," he said. "Whatever you have to say, you can say it here. I'm married now. Two kids. It took me six years to get over what you did. Everyone heard you say yes, and the next morning you were gone. All my friends, my whole family. Can you imagine how embarrassing that was?"

"That's your speech?" Cordelia asked. The memories of what had happened were flooding in, and Cordelia was angry, protective of her younger self.

"You've been practicing that for what, ten years, and it comes down to how embarrassed you were? Did you ever try to understand that young girl? She loved you. But was she ready for what you sprung on her?" The scene became clear in her memory. It had happened here, in this same house.

"Had you mentioned marriage before having a big party and proposing in front of a bunch of self-important old-South yahoos that thought she was beneath you? That talked about her clothes as if she got them all at the Salvation Army? Who told her she talked like a television announcer and not like the genteel southern lady their precious Drake Sullivan should marry? Of course she said yes, you idiot. Of course she had to leave. She could never be herself *here*." She waved her hand at the porch with the columns and the brass knockers.

A tear fell from his cheek, and he quickly wiped it away. Sarah felt the tears on her own cheeks drying slowly. Cordelia was protecting Theresa, and Cordelia was nowhere near tears. She was angry.

"Why are you back?" he asked. "Why now? Is it to get your things? Mother wanted to burn it all, but I wouldn't let her. It's all in the big steamer trunk, except for the painting. In the back of the garage."

A Distant Beacon

Theresa's personal effects. Sarah thought of the exercises, and knew she needed to see those things, to get in touch with Theresa as she had with Cordelia. She pushed Cordelia away, and held her hands up to the man in the doorway, considering what to say to change the tone.

"You're a good man, Drake," she said, in a calmer voice. "I know you've been hurt, and I'm sorry about that. I'm glad you're doing well, and congratulations on the family. You deserve it. I didn't come here to stir things up or make trouble for you. But yes, I'd love to see those things, especially the painting."

He seemed to relax a bit, and lost an inch or more in stature. Another tear fell, and was quickly wiped away. He stood back, and opened the door wide.

"Mother didn't know it was yours," he said, "or she'd never have let me keep it on the wall. I look at it every day, you know. It used to remind me of you. Now it's just a part of the house."

He walked into the living room, and stood facing a large painting above one of three fireplaces in the huge room. Sarah saw the lighthouse again, this time from a different angle, the sky a dim pre-dawn, the sea calm. The Tygaard Light. She walked up to the painting, and touched the signature. *Morganna*.

Drake Sullivan walked up next to her, and, reaching up, took the painting off the wall. The frame was heavy, and he handed it to Warwick.

"The trunk is through here," he said, walking through the big room towards another door. That door led down some stairs and into a five-car garage that was impossibly neat, as if it were a new car showroom. The floor looked polished. There was only one car, a dark sedan, gleaming under the bright lights.

Sullivan walked to the rear of the garage, and pulled aside a large sliding door that hid an assortment of sports equipment hung neatly on racks. Tennis racquets, skis, bicycle helmets. Seeming out of place was a large brown trunk, with rusted steel joints in the corners, and a rusted hasp in the front. He pulled it out by one handle onto the polished garage floor, the steel leaving scratches as it slid.

Sarah came closer and put her hand on the trunk, fingers sliding toward the hasp. She pulled the rusted metal away from the loop of steel where a lock might have once been, and opened the trunk.

Inside were some clothes, some books, both notebooks and bound textbooks, a jewelry box, a makeup case, and a few other items.

Warwick stepped closer to her. "You won't be getting that to fit in the car," he said quietly.

"I'll get you some bags," Sullivan said, walking back to the stairs.

"Thank you," Sarah said to his back, still examining the items in the trunk. There was a book of sheet music for the piano. She recognized it, and pictured playing from it on a hard bench in front of a huge grand piano, with Drake Sullivan and his friends drinking cocktails and talking over the music. She picked up one of the textbooks, and remembered college classes. History, political science, economics, statistics, calculus. Burning her shirtsleeve in a chemistry lab. Typing in the computer lab. Studying all night with a group of giggling young women whose interests were anywhere but the business law final.

Sullivan came back with several paper bags, and she began packing the items carefully, layering books and clothes around more fragile items. A ceramic squirrel she had made in an art class. A wire sculpture of a turtle she had bought at a street fair.

A Distant Beacon

When the trunk was empty, Sullivan put it back in its place, and closed the sliding doors. The garage was as it had been, except for some long scratches in the floor. He pushed a button, and one of five big doors opened noisily on tracks. The bright light of the morning overpowered the garage lights. They walked out to the Lamborghini, Warwick carrying the heavy painting, Sullivan and Sarah carrying the bags.

"Nice car," Sullivan said to Warwick as they walked past the big wrought-iron gates.

"Not mine," Warwick said, turning towards Sarah. "I've never driven a car with a stick shift."

She pushed a button on the key fob, and opened the hood in the front of the car. She carefully packed the two bags she was carrying, and reached for the two in Sullivan's hands.

"Not a lot of room in there," he said. He handed her a bag, and she laid it on its side on top of the others. The last bag she wedged in, and closed the hood.

"What are we going to do with this?" Warwick asked, holding the painting.

Sarah examined the painting carefully, then looked at the car. "We could put it on top of the engine," she said. "Might need to lose the frame."

She took the painting and examined the back. The canvas and stretcher were stapled to the frame in three places. She gripped the frame with her fingers and pushed on the stretcher board with her thumbs, and it popped out of the frame. She handed the frame to Sullivan. "You can keep that," she said.

In the end, the painting fit, just barely, behind the seats. It blocked the view from the rear view mirror, but the car had a rear-view camera display on the dash, so it wouldn't matter much.

With everything stowed, there was an awkward moment, as the three stood on the sidewalk with the car doors open.

"Is there a way I can contact you?" Sullivan asked.

"You don't think you'll be glad to be rid of me?" Sarah replied.

"It's just, I mean, in case," he said, looking at the ground.

"Enjoy your life," Sarah said. "Enjoy your wife and your two kids. Forget about Theresa Jennings, and move on. You deserve to be free of that."

She walked around to get into the car. Warwick sat down next to her and shut his door. Drake Sullivan stood on the sidewalk, the empty picture frame in one hand, and jumped a bit when she revved the big V10 engine before gliding away.

It was several minutes before Warwick said anything.

"You know, if that was private, I could have stayed in the car."

She took her hand from the gearshift knob and put it on his thigh.

"No, thanks for being there. I think it helped." Sarah realized that it had actually helped a lot. She felt comfort in knowing he was there, and she was not alone in this.

"So, is Theresa your sister? He thought you were her for a minute there."

"Yeah," Sarah said after a bit. "He did seem a little confused."

A Distant Beacon

When they got back to the hotel, Sarah didn't even pretend to offer Warwick a ride home. She handed the car off to the valet, and said, "If you're free for lunch tomorrow, I'd love some company."

"I'll make sure I'm free," he said. "Noonish?"

"Noonish," she agreed. "Oh, and before I forget, Colper Medical." She walked to the hotel door.

"What's that?" he said, calling out before she could open the door.

"For your spreadsheet. My pick. Colper Medical." She opened the door and went inside.

Chapter Six

In her room, the porter arrived with the contents of the Gallardo. She thanked him and tipped him, and set about arranging all of Theresa's belongings on the bed, and next to them those items from Cordelia she had brought along. She looked at all of the items spread out, and mentally tried to see if any of them had special memories attached.

Those of Theresa's items that had any memories at all evoked generally pleasant ones. Theresa had enjoyed college. She had friends, and she had fallen in love. It was only the end that caused any pain, and nothing arrayed on the bed reflected anything but the pleasant life of the college student.

Cordelia's tablet computer was special. She picked it up, and let Cordelia handle it. Her fingers typed out a long sentence in reply to the login query, and she said the word "Tygaard" aloud in response to the voice ID request. The screen blinked, and showed an array of icons. She was in.

She wrote a quick email to Maria in acquisitions at Tygaard Securities. *Someone is trying to manipulate the price of Portland Chemical in a pump-and-dump scheme. We're going to take their lunch money. Buy call options for half-again the latest price, and make them very popular, offer just under the current price if necessary. We want to lock it up so no one else can buy. If the price gets to half-again the latest price, sell to keep the stock below that. We want to keep the stock as stable as we can.*

Also, buy Colper Medical slowly, ramping the price up to three times the morning open over a three day period and keep it there. Then in two weeks, announce a tender offer for half that for the remainder of the company. We want to own it outright.

A Distant Beacon

Sarah watched Cordelia work, and felt pride, but also a little remorse. *Poor Douglas. He won't know what hit him. And I'm getting to like the guy. Quite a bit. He's fun, charming, and very good-looking, and completely out of his league.*

There was a lot of email to catch up on. Cordelia scanned through it, selecting canned responses for much of it, sending some replies with careful wording, and leaving a few unanswered. The rest she archived without replies. It was getting late when she finished. Sarah had let Cordelia operate the device almost on autopilot, but as she put it down, she noticed something that surprised her. The emails were going out in Wilson Bellingham's name, not Cordelia's. She turned the tablet off, moved all of the personal items off the bed, and turned down the sheets.

Once asleep, she dreamed.

A woman with no face was presenting flash cards to her, as if teaching her multiplication. The cards had names and addresses on them.

They're called safe-houses, because they'll keep you safe, the woman said. *You have to know these by heart, it is very important. Never get them mixed up. You have to be these people.*

She read the card. *Theresa Jennings, 622 Densley Drive, North Decatur, Georgia.* She knew that card by heart already. She imagined what kind of person Theresa Jennings would be. She'd be a nice person. Kind of plain, not loud or flashy.

In the morning, she wrote down the address, and looked it up on the map using Cordelia's computer. She knew the way by heart from Tuxedo Park to North Decatur. She also knew the way from Densley Drive to the university. In her mind, she wore a helmet, and she swerved between cars, leaning this way and that, on two wheels.

While waiting for lunchtime to come around, Cordelia read and answered Wilson Bellingham's emails, and Sarah practiced the guitar. Her fingers were no longer sore, and she could once again handle the intricate fingering of the more difficult pieces. In the back of her mind, she was transposing the music to the piano.

A little before noon, she was in the hotel lobby, anxious to get going. When she saw Douglas Warwick walking towards the glass hotel doors, she jumped from her seat and almost ran to meet him.

She dangled the Gallardo keys in front of him. "You want to drive?" she asked.

"I don't know how to work a stick shift," he said.

"Then don't," she said. "It's got over 500 horsepower, you can put it fifth or sixth gear and just go. Not as much fun, but probably a lot safer."

He shook his head. "If it's all right with you, I think I'd be more comfortable as a passenger."

"OK, chicken," she said playfully. The valet had brought the car out 20 minutes earlier, and he followed her and got in.

"Are you hungry?" she asked. "I didn't check to see if it's still there, but we'll just see when we get there. It's a nice place I remember, all kinds of beer if you like, but I used to go there for the pierogis. They also had a kick-ass curry."

A Distant Beacon

"Sounds great," he said. "What's special about Colper Medical?" he added, changing the subject.

"Nothing, yet," she said, noncommittally.

"Portland Chemical is up an eighth," he said. "Colper hasn't moved."

"And West Texas Crude is falling," she replied. "I checked them all this morning too."

It didn't take long to get to the Brick Store Pub in Decatur. And the pierogis were everything she had remembered. Warwick had a craft beer and some fish and chips. Sarah was anxious to get going, and ate quickly, then helped him finish his French fries.

"There's a stop we need to make," she said. "It's not far from here."

"I got the impression we didn't come out this way just for lunch," Warwick said.

"But you didn't pry," she said. "I like that in a guy."

"You're private," he said. "I get that. But then you open up completely, all of a sudden. Sometimes it's like you're two different people."

"Or more," she said, under her breath.

She drove to Densley Drive without needing the car's navigation system. The house was well kept-up, in a neighborhood that generally wasn't. She pulled the Gallardo into the driveway, and walked up to the big garage door. Sarah held the combination lock in her hand until her fingers found the right numbers. *36-14-24. Barbie-doll figure.*

The lock fell open, and she removed it. The garage door had no automatic controls; she pulled it open with a strong tug, and it swung upwards.

Her Vespa scooter stood in the center of the garage, both tires flat, the whole thing covered in a layer of dust. She moved it to one side of the otherwise empty garage, and went back to pull the Gallardo into the garage. It wasn't a car you could leave unattended on the street without attracting attention.

She closed the garage door from the inside, and opened the unlocked door to the little kitchen. Warwick followed her in, and together they walked through the neatly kept house. Sarah noticed the nail in the wall where the painting had hung. Instead of the mail bins that she had found when she had returned from the hospital, here there was a large barrel, half-full of mail. With Warwick's help, she rolled it into the living room and dumped the contents onto the floor in front of the old couch.

She directed Warwick as they started sorting the mail. "Bank statements here, anything that looks like a bill here, anything with a hand-written address here," she said, pointing to spots on the floor. She picked up one of the hand-addressed envelopes. "And anything from a Sullivan goes here," she said, carefully placing the letter up on the couch.

Warwick picked through the pile, looking for bank statements and bills, leaving anything that might be personal for Sarah to handle. He neatly arranged the mail in stacks by postmark date.

Sarah closed her eyes and mentally walked through the routines in the leather-bound notebook that were supposed to bring back Theresa's memories. Establish a timeline.

Well, we know when we left Atlanta.

A Distant Beacon

That was one end of the timeline. Theresa had gone to college here. Memories of college life were accessible. Classes, with the piano and music theory classes, mathematics, business law, they all came easily. Less easy were memories of time with Drake Sullivan. He hadn't been her first love. People found Theresa easily approachable, and unintimidating. They opened up to her. *Now I know when we lost our virginity.*

Loss. Overwhelmingly, that is what she felt from Theresa. Unlike the others, Theresa had lost friends and people she loved. She was more of a real person than Cordelia or Sarah; she had connections to the world. And she had lost them all.

She opened her eyes, and picked up a letter. Not from the pile of letters from Drake and his family. This one was from a friend, a classmate. She started to open it, but found she could barely see through tears. She put her hands and the letter down in her lap and closed her eyes again. The tears would not stop.

The sound of Warwick carefully sorting letters stopped, and she heard him scoot over next to her on the floor. His arm went around her shoulders.

"I'm sorry," she said.

"Don't be," he replied. "It's OK. Just let it happen. Sometimes you just need to cry."

She leaned back against the couch, her head facing the ceiling, and tried to wipe away the tears but they just kept coming. She could feel Theresa's heartache, and she realized that the escape from Atlanta was not the end of Theresa's timeline. Theresa had come back one evening at Cordelia's big house, and had realized what she had lost. The half-hearted suicide attempt in the pool, interrupted by Peter Thompson, had taught her she couldn't fix things that way. She had left a note for Cordelia. Somehow, they had to communicate, to get back together. Or one day one of them would actually succeed at ending it all.

It was Cordelia who awoke the next morning and read the message scrawled in ballpoint pen on her thigh. That is what started the quest that ended up at Montgomery General.

Cordelia's memories from that day forward were now accessible, and Sarah sat forward, eyes wide open.

"I know all about Wilson Bellingham," she said. "I know why no one can find him."

"So he's alive?" Warwick asked.

Sarah got out the words, "No, I'm afraid not," before Cordelia stopped her. "But that's all I can say about it. Don't ask again."

Her cold tone caused him to draw away. "Sorry," he said. "I'll go back to being that guy who doesn't pry."

Sarah pulled him back and hugged him hard. "I'm really glad you're here," she said. "I really can't be alone right now. There's just too much to take in. I'm sorry I've been so messed up."

"Don't worry about it," he said, adjusting himself to her arms. She loosened her grip on him, and pulled back just enough to look him in the face, from very close. It took him completely by surprise when she leaned in and kissed him, a long, slow, warm kiss that once he recovered, he returned gently. They sat locked together for a moment, and when the kiss ended, she still held on.

"Do you have to be somewhere tonight?" she asked. "Because I was thinking, we could just stay here tonight. It's a big bed, you know. Plenty of room for two."

A Distant Beacon

"Um," he started, "I — have no plans," he got out before her lips clamped on his again, her mouth slightly open. It was a while this time before she let up.

~

That night she dreamed about the woman without a face again. This time there were no flash cards. There was urgency in her voice. *Hide in the skiff. Whatever happens, don't make a sound. Not a peep, no matter what.*

She was in a small boat, towed behind a much larger craft, and the woman was pulling a damp tarp over her. The woman with no face let out the rope that held the small boat, and Sarah watched her recede until the rope tightened. She was peeking from under the tarp, just a bare crack of a view. She could hear the loud roar of another craft approaching, and feel the world rock from its wake.

The sails on the big catamaran were full with wind, but they were no match for the fast motor launch. The powerboat came up alongside the sailboat, and four men jumped aboard. The dark of the evening lit up suddenly as the thunder of automatic weapons fire rang out over the water. The woman screamed and ran towards the man at the helm of the sailboat as he collapsed, and the boat turned into the wind. The big sails shook like thunder, and more flashes came as the gunfire roared over the sound of the angry sails. Sarah gripped the sides of the little boat until her hands ached, but she did not cry out or move.

She hadn't seen the woman go down. The image of the man slumped at the helm transfixed her, and fear battled with pain and loss as she watched the scene unfold. The four men poured something onto the deck of the sailboat, and climbed quickly back into the speedboat. A flare-gun made a sharp report, and the sailboat was quickly ablaze. The shaking sails caught fire and the night was suddenly bright as day, and Sarah could hear the sound of the powerboat racing off into the night.

"What is it?" Warwick asked, suddenly awakened by Sarah sitting up quickly in bed, breathing in gasps as she whimpered in fear.

A Distant Beacon

She grabbed him and held him tight as she regained her breath. "I watched him die," she said. "I watched him die."

~

In the morning, neither of them spoke about what had happened in the middle of the night. Warwick was determined not to pry, and Sarah content to ignore the event altogether, at least as far as discussing it. However, it continued to haunt her throughout the day. She dropped Warwick off at the hotel, and drove around Atlanta aimlessly, trying to fit the vivid image into her timeline. It wasn't one of Theresa's memories, of that she was sure. Cordelia had never had that experience either.

Morganna.

The picture of the lighthouse. It was always viewed from out at sea, in all the paintings.

> *I know I'm home when weary eyes first sight,*
> *The distant beacon of the Tygaard light.*

The man at the helm of the sailboat had quoted that poem to her. He kept that book of sea poems on the shelf next to the marine radio, where he could read it to her on long stretches between ports. However, like the woman, he had no face.

It became difficult to see the road as her eyes teared up again, and she pulled over to the side of the road. The timeline. When had that night on the sailboat happened? Early. Before Theresa, Sarah, or Cordelia. The terrified young woman in the skiff was barely old enough to drive, but when the burning rope set the skiff adrift, she knew exactly what to do. They had prepared her for this. They had drilled her in how to deal with exactly this situation.

They're called safe-houses, because they'll keep you safe.

Sarah Johnson, Cordelia Watson, Theresa Jennings. There was a house for each of them, money to live on, birth certificates, identification, and histories. First, get ashore, sink the skiff, and

A Distant Beacon

disappear. You can't be that person anymore. She didn't want to be. She needed to forget.

Chapter Seven

Jonas Reynolds sat in an interview room in the Atlanta police station. Next to him were two Atlanta detectives. Across the table from them was a young man in a cheap suit known by many names in the papers in front of Reynolds, the most recent being Douglas Warwick.

One of the Atlanta detectives was speaking. "Detective Reynolds here has flown all the way out from California to talk to you. You might want to listen very carefully to what he has to say. You might say your future depends a lot on whether you can be of any assistance to him." The tone was mocking and condescending. Warwick had heard it before. He said nothing, but looked at Reynolds.

"I need Cordelia Bellingham," Reynolds said. "We know you have been targeting her for a stock scam. Your buddy in the other room says you're the one who made contact. I need to know where she is, and whether she is armed."

"I think you have the wrong person," Warwick said. "All I know about the woman is what I've seen on television."

The detectives looked at one another for a moment. Then Reynolds spoke again. "You're in Georgia," he said. "You aren't in New York anymore. In Georgia, if you are convicted of a felony, and you have been previously convicted of a felony anywhere in the U.S., say in New York, for example, then you get the maximum sentence provided by law. They don't wait for a third strike here, although they have that too — no parole at all for the third time."

"But I haven't been convicted of a felony in Georgia," Warwick said. "I haven't even been arrested."

"Well, about that," the first detective said. "There's this little thing called stock manipulation."

"It's against the law to lose money in the stock market?" Warwick asked.

"You seem to have lost quite a bit of money," the condescending tone continued. "At least your buddy says you will, when some options expire tomorrow. Unless something happens to the value of a certain stock you've been placing bets on. All those bets should have pumped that baby way up by now. But nothing has happened; the price has been solid as a rock. I'll bet that really pisses you off."

"So you're arresting me for failing to manipulate a stock?" Warwick asked.

The detectives looked at one another again. This time the condescending one had nothing to say.

Reynolds stepped in. "Attempted manipulation is still a felony," he said. "You don't want to take that chance."

"Maybe I should," Warwick said. "It sounds like a pretty weak case. I'm pretty sure you didn't pick me up just to discuss that."

"I told you," Reynolds said. "I just want the Bellingham woman."

"And you think I know where she is," Warwick finished for him.

"Atlanta P.D. has been tracking you two since a woman reported being defrauded of a rather large amount of money in what she suspected was a swindle of some kind," Reynolds said. "And you know that if she had kept better records you two would already be locked up for it. That would be your buddy's third strike, too. But he cut a deal. He's been telling these nice gentlemen all about your latest scam, and when they heard that Bellingham was the target,

I got a call. Now these guys have been waiting for that stock to jump so they can catch you red-handed, but somehow that hasn't turned out the way any of us expected it to. So we're talking to you now."

"With some kind of a deal," Warwick said. "Because you have a shit case that's falling apart, and Larry's no good to you because he doesn't know squat."

Condescending tone stood up. "Listen you," he said, but Reynolds pulled him down.

"Let's approach this from a less adversarial viewpoint," he said. "I didn't come here to arrest *you*. I'm asking you for a favor. Let me know where to find her. In return, anything you say here will be off the record, the detectives here won't arrest you for anything, and you won't have to pay for attorneys and bail with money you no longer have. And you won't run the risk that a jury decides they just don't like New York felons playing games in their nice city."

"And he leaves Georgia," condescending said, "for good."

"If I knew this lady," Warwick said. "Why would I give her up, deal or no deal? What's she ever done to me?"

"Nothing yet," Reynolds said. "But she has just come from a mental institution, where she was being treated for some kind of multiple personality disease. And we have evidence that she has killed at least two people — a janitor named Arthur Woods, and her husband, Wilson Bellingham."

"She killed him?" Warwick asked.

"We're pretty certain of both of those cases," Reynolds said. "But there may be more. Has Mrs. Bellingham ever seemed to you to be, how would I say it, 'unbalanced'? Like one minute she was one

A Distant Beacon

person and the next minute she was someone else? Any sudden mood swings?"

Warwick sat and said nothing. The three detectives looked at one another again. Reynolds kept trying.

"You may personally be at risk," he said. "She kills without motive. Have you ever been alone with her, away from public places, where she might have an opportunity to kill you? And the other thing I need to know — have you seen her with any weapons? Or anything she might keep a gun in, that she always carries with her?"

"You mean like a violin case or something?" Warwick asked. Then he thought about the guitar case and how he had never seen her open it.

"Is she carrying a violin case?" Reynolds asked.

Warwick heard the eagerness in the detective's question. "You watch too many gangster movies," he said. "You think you're Eliot Ness."

~

Sarah woke late, and stayed in bed trying to remember as much of the dream as she could. She wrote in the notebook all the items she could list. Focusing on the transition between Theresa and Sarah had helped a lot in bringing back Theresa's memories. Focusing on the transition from Morganna to Theresa might also bring back Morganna's memories, but those were so frightening and painful that only fragmented images came, there was no sense of time, no indication of which events happened in which order.

Letting Cordelia handle business dealings had helped to access Cordelia's memories. Playing the piano had helped to access Theresa. Letting Morganna do the things that she was good at might help to bring *her* past to life.

She got out of bed and got the knee-high boots from the closet. Undoing the long laces, she began tying different sailor's knots in the string. A bowline, a sheet bend, a bowline on a bight, a Carrick bend. She remembered her father demonstrating the knots, quizzing her on where and when she could use them. The salt air, the chill of the spray, the feeling of speed as the wake boiled noisily past the rudders.

The Quest out of Long Beach. That was the name of the boat. Mom in the galley cooking something. Lying on the hammock between the twin hulls, missing the heeling of the single-hulled boat she had learned to sail on, the sense of knowing you were speeding by the tilt of the deck.

The faces wouldn't come. They were just mom and dad. His fingers callused as he wove the ropes in her hands. He was so smart; he always knew how to figure anything out. Working out math problems, teaching her how to navigate with a sextant. Mom brushing her daughter's hair. Helping her deal with acne embarrassment. Selecting her first bra. Mom's pride in her drawings.

A Distant Beacon

Of course.

Sarah got the pad of paper from beside the phone, and held her pen in her hand, wondering how to let Morganna draw. But her hand was already working, quickly sketching an oval in light strokes, repeatedly, then a plus sign in the middle of the oval, which turned into eyes, a nose, and a mouth. A face began to emerge from the light traces of ink. A Hispanic looking face, with a scar from the forehead down to the cheek, across the left eye. The man on *The Quest*, the one with the automatic rifle who had poured gasoline on the deck.

She could not remember her parents' faces, but this face from years ago was carved into her memory permanently. Her hands kept working on the drawing, detailing ears, hair, chin, things she was sure were not actually memories, but just the practiced skill of an artist with experience in drawing portraits.

The drawing was quite good, and this surprised and delighted Sarah, who would otherwise have been certain that she had no artistic talent whatsoever. She felt no emotion when she looked at the face, as if this was only some villain from a movie from long ago. Morganna had gone as soon as she finished the drawing.

She showered and dressed, and went downstairs to the piano in the lobby, hoping to bring Morganna back through her music. She sat on the bench, touching the keys. The lobby was quiet, the morning crowd gone, the lunch crowd not yet arrived, and she was reluctant to attract attention to herself right now. She gently pressed a key, trying to be quiet, and the sound quickly cut short as she lifted her finger from the key. She looked in the mirror, to where she had first seen Douglas Warwick, sneaking a hand into her purse. There was no one there.

I know it's just the treatment. Be cautious of sudden attractions to people, your brain is still plastic. But it feels so nice, so right.

It seemed strange that Warwick had not contacted her. Was this normal after sleeping together the first time? She thought not. Shouldn't he be even more eager to be with her? Or was it that he was rethinking his plans to take her money and disappear? It seemed unlikely that he would be able to complete his scam. By her reckoning, he had probably spent all he could afford trying to make that stock move, as there had been no recent attempts at manipulation.

Maybe he had already cut his losses, and left town. Their night together had meant nothing to him, just an unexpected bonus; an expensive one-night stand he would try to forget. That would be sad; she was certain her feelings for him were genuine. In the days they had spent together, he had become more than the game. That night had been more than her need for comfort. She had wanted him. She still wanted him.

She pressed another key on the piano, holding it down and letting the sound slowly fade away. She tried not to think about Douglas, but to concentrate on Morganna. When had she learned to play the piano? Her fingers on the keys told her Morganna never had. Theresa was the piano player, she must have learned in college, or just before. To reach Morganna she would need knots, sailing, or art.

She looked up art supplies on her phone, and was about to walk out of the hotel to find the valet and get the car when she noticed the nearest art supply store was only a short walk. She waved at the valet, and continued walking, out onto the sidewalk. She looked for Douglas, half-expecting to find him walking towards the hotel, but he was nowhere to be found.

The store was quaint, smelling of oil paint and turpentine, and had easels set up in the back, and a small stage for models, but no classes were being held at the moment. She nodded at the lone clerk at the register, and walked past, scanning the walls where

A Distant Beacon

empty frames were hung with price tags, and the small aisles stacked with brushes, paint tubes, stretched and sized canvases, and arrays of pens and nibs.

She selected a few charcoal pencils and a large drawing pad, letting Morganna choose. A set of colored pencils, some pastel crayons, a fine line-drawing pen. Morganna's delight in being able to select anything she wanted reminded Sarah of a child in a toy store.

She checked out, and walked back to the hotel with a large bag of art supplies, but her attention was on the street, looking for a particular face. Douglas was not on the street, and he was not in the hotel lobby. The clerk at the desk had not seen him either.

Back in her room, she spent the afternoon drawing in charcoal on the large art pad. The faces of the men on the boat took shape, the one with the scar, and the one she thought she had seen with her father in the house sometime in the year before the incident on the water. Nothing came when she tried to steer Morganna to draw her parents' faces.

A sketch of the boat revealed details she would never have remembered from a dream. The way the ropes were coiled and stored, the shape of the anchor, the way the sails were set, the net mesh between the hulls in the bow. Even the tell-tales at the top of the sail that indicated wind direction came back to her as her fingers moved back and forth across the page, leaving subtle strokes of black and grey on the paper.

As the afternoon faded away into evening, the big pad was nearly half-exhausted, as was Sarah. Her fingers and hands were smudged black with charcoal, the gray smudges were everywhere, on her clothes, on her face, on her arms, and all over the nice upholstered chair she had been sitting in. She was starving, having skipped lunch, but she needed another shower and a change of clothes.

In the bathroom, she saw the streaks of black under her eyes, and realized she had been crying as she drew. She had not noticed. It took a long time to get all of the black dust off her skin, and as she dried off, she checked the white towel carefully for evidence of any she had missed. She brushed and dried her hair, and dressed for dinner, examining the array of drawings strewn about the room as she did. Each one held a clue to memories that were just below the surface, hesitant, shy memories that needed gentle encouragement to come forward.

Back down in the lobby she once again looked around, hoping to see Douglas Warwick's familiar face on the way to the hotel restaurant. He did not appear. She ordered a huge meal, and wolfed it down hungrily, as if she had to eat for a week and rush off quickly. When she was finally quite stuffed, and resisting the impish impulse to emit a loud belch that would awaken and startle the other diners in the quiet room, she found she had nowhere to go. She sat at the table, not wanting to go back to her room, but not wanting to leave the hotel.

She kept looking for Douglas as people walked by the glass doors. She watched the other diners quietly discussing whatever had brought them together, or brought them here, wondering if that pair were new lovers, or that pair were starting a new business. Life was happening all around her, and she was separate, cocooned in her corner, watching it all go by. Alone.

She missed him. She didn't want him to walk away, to forget her. Sarah had always been alone, not making close friends, not having lovers. Cordelia had been aloof; all of those close to her were business partners or employees, always kept in their categories, labeled and distinct, unemotional and efficient. The new combination of Sarah/Cordelia/Theresa was more open, and

A Distant Beacon

needed human contact, wanted someone to love and care for. The cautious Morganna was afraid of strangers, but needed family, wanted friendships.

All of the parts of her were merging into one. Doctor Williams would be proud. It was exactly the result he had hoped for, with his notebook of exercises, his drugs and neurosurgery. But the key was finding what each part of her loved the most, was the best at, and using those as rewards to bring each one out of the past and into the present. She would have to show him how to re-write his little book.

The restaurant was thinning out, and the waiter had given up on returning to her table, having left the bill long ago. She left cash with the bill, including a large tip, and stood up, looking once more around the room. She continued to search every face as she entered the lobby. The desk clerk saw the question on her face from thirty feet away and simply shook her head as a negative.

She took the elevator to her room, and carefully moved the drawings off the bed, placing some on the desk, some on the dresser, and some on the chair. They would give up their secrets another time. She undressed and slipped under the cold sheets, and was asleep in minutes.

Chapter Eight

"Ms. Waterston?" the voice behind the door asked, after a brief knock.

Sarah was already up, showered, and dressed, and had been considering whether to start another day of drawing, maybe using the colored pastels this time, to see if color helped bring more memories, or brought more emotions. She held a charcoal pencil in her hand, half consumed by the previous day's efforts.

She opened the door, and said, "Yes?" before noticing the three men behind the male desk clerk, two of them in uniform. The men pushed past him quickly, entering the room and surrounding Sarah.

"Cordelia Bellingham," said the one in plain clothes, "You are under arrest for the murders of Arthur Woods and Wilson Bellingham." At the sound of her name, Cordelia took charge, and her body straightened until it was clear that she was taller than the two uniformed men beside her were, but not nearly as tall as the man with the California accent. She was about to tell them all how ridiculous their accusations were, but Reynolds was advising her of her rights. She had the right to remain silent, and that was going to be exactly what she did, until she had a swarm of lawyers to do her talking for her.

"I invoke my right to counsel," she said to the tall man, as she folded her arms in front of her, giving the officer with the handcuffs a withering look. Reynolds waved him away, and he put the cuffs back into their place on his belt. The five of them rode the elevator to the lobby, and the three men escorted her out the front door. Two police cars had parked in the valet area, and she could see Douglas Warwick in the back seat of one of them. When he saw her, he avoided her eyes, looking down at his feet.

A Distant Beacon

Her heart sank as they led her to the other car, and she batted away the hand that one of them placed on her head to guide her in.

"You need to pick a better class of friends," Reynolds said as he slipped into the front passenger seat. He nodded towards Warwick in the other car. "He brought us right to you."

She said nothing. On the drive to the police station, the otherwise icy quiet was continually broken by the traffic on the police radio, and Reynolds seldom let his eyes leave his prisoner in the back seat. He studied her carefully for the entire ride.

When they arrived, the driver insisted on the handcuffs, and all three men led her into the building, her hands in front of her, feeling unnatural. She held the metal cuffs hidden with her hands as best she could, and tried to walk normally. She was fingerprinted and processed, and allowed to phone Jameson, who told her to say nothing, and that legal help was on its way and should be with her in minutes.

The cell door closed with a metallic bang. There were two other women in the cell, and one of them stretched out fully on the only bench, eyes closed. The standing woman glanced at Sarah briefly, and then stared out the bars at the bare wall.

She thought about Douglas in the car. *He brought us right to you.* Her eyes began to tear up, but Cordelia clamped down hard, jaw clenched. *Not here. Not now.*

Almost an hour passed before a young man in an expensive suit was escorted to her cell. He handed her his business card. "The senior partner is before the judge as we speak," he said. "They are trying to deny bail. Besides the murder charge, they are saying you fled once, and are clearly a flight risk. Since you hadn't been arrested, we don't think they can make that stick. But it might not matter anyway, since detective Reynolds has asked for your release into his custody for return to California, and from what I can gather, he is in no mood to stay any longer in Georgia than he can."

"So," Cordelia said, "no bail, but economy class with a gorilla in the middle seat all the way to LAX."

He nodded. "I'm afraid it may be a few hours yet."

"How soon can you bail these two out?" Sarah said, waving at her cellmates. The one on the bench opened her eyes, and the one standing looked over at her. "I'd like my privacy," Cordelia said to the lawyer, "But see they get the best representation." She looked at the standing woman. "My treat."

"I'll do that," the young lawyer said. He waited for Cordelia to say something more, but she waved him away impatiently. "Right away," he said, walking quickly ahead of the officer he had come in with.

When they had gone, the standing woman turned to Sarah. "What is it, Miss Fancy Dress, I smell bad or something?"

Sarah prevented Cordelia from making a sharp remark, and took over. "You don't belong here," she said. "Nobody does. I'm being an asshole so you know you don't owe me anything. I just want to be alone."

"But you're getting lawyers for both of us," the woman said, leaning back against the bars.

Sarah considered this, and then said, "Anything that pisses off the Atlanta police is worth it."

The woman thought about that quietly, and then turned away. "Then I guess we'll give you some privacy," she said, and kicked the foot of the woman on the bench. The second woman rose, and

A Distant Beacon

the two of them walked silently back to the corner of the cell where the standing woman had been. Sarah walked over to the bench and sat down, leaned her back against the cold wall, and closed her eyes.

Less than ten minutes had gone by before two more young men in expensive suits were escorted to the cell, and the two women were out on bail. Sarah stood to watch them all walk down the hallway, and out the door at the end. Then she sat back down on the bench for a long wait. She allowed herself to cry quietly, thinking of Douglas in the back seat of the patrol car.

So, Arthur Woods is dead, and it's your fault. You knew you were a killer.

She wondered how he had died.

Reynolds and an older lawyer came to the cell a few hours later. The senior partner of the law firm Jameson had hired spoke to Sarah alone in an interview room at the police station. "I'm Jack Lawrence," the man said. "I'll be accompanying you two to California," he said. "I've upgraded us to first class, by the way. I'd advise against saying anything to the detective. You can talk to me, but we should not discuss any details of the case, or any of your actions or motives, when the detective can hear. Maybe we can find something to talk about, like music or theater or something, or I can arrange to have some music for you and you can just get some rest."

"That would be nice," she said.

"Your people will meet us at the airport, but the police there will be taking you on alone to Santa Barbara. Again I would advise against saying anything to anyone without your lawyer present."

She nodded.

"There is one option at this point. Technically, you are not a fugitive, since you were already in Georgia when the indictment was made in California. We have the legal right to contest extradition, should you so choose. It is the advice of my team, and your law firm in California, that you waive this right and return to Santa Barbara. Do you understand?"

"I do," Sarah said. "I have no further business in Atlanta."

"Do you have any questions?" he asked.

"My phone, my drawings, my guitar, my computer?" she asked.

"They are being packed separately, as evidence. If you need to communicate with someone, it should be through me." He finished, but she had nothing more to say. "Is there anything I can get you for the flight?"

"A pencil," she said, "and a sketch pad."

"You mean like an artist's pad, for drawing?"

She nodded.

"I'll have those brought to us at the airport," he said.

Reynolds was waiting outside the door when they left, and the three of them walked out of the station to where a limousine was waiting to take them to the airport. Reynolds examined it as if he'd never been in one before as they all entered. He seemed uncomfortable. Lawrence noticed this, and broke the ice.

"Have you been enjoying your stay in Atlanta?" he asked the detective.

The detective grunted. "If there was a cheaper motel, they would have found it for me," he said. "But hey, a bed is a bed."

"Well," Lawrence continued, "at least your return flight should be more comfortable than the flight here."

"I don't mind economy class," Reynolds said, settling in.

"That's where we differ," the lawyer replied. "And I expect you might change your mind by the end of the trip. For a man of your stature, the extra legroom alone should be most welcome."

Reynolds grunted again, and said nothing for the rest of the ride to the airport.

Once at the airport, yet another young man in an expensive suit met them with tickets and a cardboard tray with coffees and pastry. At Lawrence's insistence, Reynolds accepted both, and added so much cream and sugar that Sarah expected him to spill the nearly overflowing cup as he stirred. She wondered to herself if he had ever had good coffee that didn't need to be so badly treated.

Just before boarding time, another young suit rushed up with a large plastic bag that held Sarah's sketchpad and a selection of pencils. Reynolds inspected the contents before handing it to Lawrence, who held it until they were seated on the plane.

They waited while the other passengers boarded. Reynolds played with the seat controls and swiveled the chair. Sarah merely belted in and sat back, closing her eyes. When the plane was ready to take off, she opened them and stared out the window, enjoying the feeling of being pressed back into the chair, and feeling the wheels leave the ground. Atlanta receded below them, and she didn't stop watching until they ascended through the clouds and there was nothing left to see.

Lawrence used the side table to arrange his papers, and began reading, using a notepad occasionally to record his thoughts.

Sarah, sitting beside him, opened the bag and brought out the sketchpad, and a soft pencil. The pencils had all been neatly sharpened and returned to their boxes.

Reynolds sat opposite them, facing the lawyer. Sarah studied his face, and he pretended to ignore her, watching the screen above their heads. She began to sketch. It was interesting to see what Morganna saw when she drew. Subtle things like the play of light on strands of graying hair, the stubble of a beard, a crease in the earlobe that Theresa recognized as a hereditary sign of heart disease risk.

As she drew, she noticed things about the man. He did not smoke. It showed in his teeth, and in the color of his skin. She did not know which of her personas knew how to tell. The tiny scab from shaving told her he used a razor, rather than an electric shaver. That was uncommon these days, as the electric devices had gotten so good. His shirt was cotton, and had not been pressed, and had not been packed gently in his carry-on bag. The small stain on the cuff might be ketchup or marinara.

She continued to sketch, catching the small wrinkles at the corners of his eyes, the details of the patterns in his iris, the lines at the corners of his mouth. These were all things she would never have given a second thought, or even noticed.

If he was married, he did not wear a ring. It had been at least three weeks since his hair had been cut, judging from the shape of the cut at the back of his neck. The hairs were no longer cut to the same length, and she could see the length difference between those hairs that were in the growth stage and those that were not.

He was fit. The shape of his shoulders and arms were from muscle, not fat, and he had no fat deposits under his chin. His nails were trimmed, but not filed. She could see corners where nail clippers had been used. The cuticles were nearly invisible, and she guessed that he showered daily, which kept them soft. He had not washed his hands since breakfast.

Lawrence stopped what he was doing and looked over at the sketch. "That's amazing," he said. "You're really good at that."

She looked at him, saying nothing, and then quickly added a narrow mustache under his nose, and a swastika patch on his arm. Lawrence snickered, and went back to his reading.

Sarah folded the cover back over the sketchpad and put it back in its bag. She reclined her chair, and closed her eyes, enjoying the sense of power the noisy engines gave the plane, and the occasional bump or tilt that told her they were actually flying through the air. She imagined a hole between her feet, where she could drop her pencils one by one to the earth below. Would they land point first? Would they pierce rooftops and stick in hardwood floors?

She woke when the jet began its descent. Looking out the window, she could see mountains and farms below. The brown horizon of Los Angeles was still ahead. Slowly, the features below became more distinct as they got closer, and then faded away again as they entered the hazy city atmosphere. All the electric cars in the world could do nothing about the inversion layer.

She felt the landing gear come down, and the flaps open up, and the hard bump as they touched down, followed by the rush of the engines reversing. She smiled. She loved takeoffs, and she loved landings.

More police met them as they deplaned, and took her to a police car for the ride to Santa Barbara. Reynolds sat beside her. She noticed a spot he had missed when shaving, just behind the jaw line. She noted the fuzz on the outside of his ear, and the little hairs on the inside. Reynolds and the driver talked during the trip, but neither one tried to engage her in their discussion.

Jameson and an army of suits met the car as it arrived at the station. "We brought you a change of clothes," Jameson said. "Judge Ramsay is already meeting with our legal team and the prosecutor, and they are all waiting for your arrival, so we're going directly to court. The thing with Wilson was bad enough, but this Arthur Woods development has us all stumped. I'll need you to fill us in on that as soon as you can."

"We'll need Doctor Williams," Sarah said. "He can tell you about Woods. I'm afraid we might be in trouble there."

Jameson seemed surprised. He studied her face. "We'll talk later," he said. "Right now, you need to change. There's a female officer that needs to accompany you while you do, and Reynolds will be with us on the ride to the courthouse." He handed her a suit in a zippered plastic bag, holding it by the hanger. She took it, and Jameson signaled to the woman in the hall as he opened the interview room door.

Another limousine met them when she came out in her court suit. The car was much nicer than the first, and Reynolds seemed to notice every special detail. Jameson leaned towards Sarah.

"Williams is on his way," he said in a whisper. "He said he couldn't talk to me about," he stopped, shifting his eyes towards Reynolds, "anyway, I'm still in the dark. He said he could talk to you, though."

She nodded.

"The other matter is tricky. I don't know how much we'll have to give up to make it go away. The tax issues I think we've kept clear, so there shouldn't be any federal involvement. The statute of

A Distant Beacon

limitations has expired on most of the serious issues, as you know, since we notified the court years ago. There are still the public relations to worry about, and we could be in for stockholder lawsuits if the stock takes a hit on any news. We have a team running scenarios, but they are still mostly in the dark on purpose, to avoid any leaks. It's a tricky business, and I can't guarantee we won't take some big lumps."

She nodded again, and squeezed his hand briefly.

"The procedure works," she told him. "I can access early memories. Some things are starting to make sense. Some of the memories are really awful. Michael, *I watched him die*."

"Watched who die?" Reynolds asked, and Sarah realized she had forgotten he was there, and had said the last sentence aloud. Jameson shook his head, so she would not answer.

"This is a privileged conversation," he said to Reynolds. The detective was having none of it.

"I can't un-hear what someone said right in front of me," he said.

They said nothing more in the car. When they reached the courthouse, a group of tall young men in suits formed a phalanx with Sarah and Jameson in the middle, and they left Reynolds standing by the car looking around for anyone he knew. He followed the group, trying to get close, but he could not even see the top of Sarah's head.

Judge Richard Ramsay did not let on that he had a close personal friendship with Cordelia Bellingham, or that she was a major donor to his campaign fund. He was all official business. He allowed Jameson and Sarah to be briefed by the legal team that had been arguing for bail, but insisted on no more than a ten-minute recess for it to be done.

"We'll get full discovery briefs now that Mrs. Bellingham is back," a tall grey haired lawyer explained. "But for now they are claiming they have witnesses that will attest to Mrs. Bellingham having confessed to two murders in their presence. They have the records of her treatment at Montgomery General, which they are arguing is evidence of a dangerous state of mind. They are claiming that the trip to Atlanta was fleeing in anticipation of arrest, and indicates a future flight risk."

Jameson had heard this already, earlier in the day. "Have they named their witnesses?" he asked.

"They have not, but it will be in the discovery packet," the older man said.

"What is your feel for our chances at bail?" Jameson asked.

"It's a murder case," the older man said. "Denial of bail is usually automatic."

Jameson turned to Sarah. "You know the judge better than any of us," he said. "What is your feeling?"

Sarah reflected on Cordelia's history with the judge, and thought for a moment. "Dick won't want to recuse himself," she said. "He will want as much control as he can keep. That will mean giving the prosecution no room to challenge. I'm afraid that means he'll give them what they want, unless we give him some kind of out."

Jameson frowned. "I don't think you're going to like the options we have much more than you'd like jail. I think any way we work this is going to have negative effects on the stock. We may be spending a lot of time in court just trying to keep the company, quite aside from our current legal problems."

A Distant Beacon

Jameson looked up at the older lawyer. The man responded by sliding a single sheet of paper across the table. Jameson slid it in front of Sarah. "This is what we've prepared."

Sarah read the paper. "Oh, shit," she said quietly. She turned the page over, blank side up, and slid it back across the table to him. "Do you think you can sell that?" she asked.

"If I can make it look like their idea," Jameson said, "Ramsay can jump on it. But it's a long shot."

"Time," the older man said, and they all stood up and walked back into the courtroom.

"Your honor," Jameson said to the judge, "The prosecution's case is hearsay, circumstantial, and weak at that. Mrs. Bellingham is not a dangerous person. She has close ties to the community, and bail can be set to ensure she has ample incentive to make all mandated court appearances. We will be open to discuss any reasonable amounts the prosecution might come up with, but it is our feeling that our client should be released on her own recognizance."

The prosecutor quickly rose. "We have witnesses to two confessions," he said. "The defendant is indeed dangerous, as her current mental condition, as evidenced by her own doctors in sworn testimony, is one where she can at any moment turn to an entirely separate personality, with its own memories, and its own moral compass. The woman is capable of killing without motive, and then not remembering having done so. She is a risk not only of flight to avoid prosecution, but to the public at large."

Jameson replied. "The prosecution is arguing that our client is in an unstable and unreliable state of mind, and at the same time that in that state of mind she has confessed to murder. We don't see how they can have it both ways. Is she a credible witness, or a danger to herself or others?"

"She can be both," the prosecutor said. "In discussions mere moments ago, in front of detective Reynolds, she was heard to say, 'I watched him die'. This is in addition to the other two admissions we have witnesses to."

Ramsay looked to Jameson. "Is this true?" he asked.

"The prosecutor is now arguing for a psychiatric hold, your honor. We strongly object to that move. This is a bail hearing. Our client belongs at home in her own bed, not locked in the secure wing of Montgomery General with a guard at the door." Jameson turned to face the prosecutor, hands on his hips in indignation.

"Mr. Jameson," the judge said, sitting taller in his chair. "I decide what this hearing is or is not. As the prosecution is making its case rather strongly for a finding of incapacity, it seems to the court that Montgomery General is exactly the place to discover the mental state of the defendant. The prosecution will decide whether they wish to supply a guard or rely on electronic monitoring. A 72 hour psychiatric hold is hereby in effect for evaluating the mental state of Mrs. Bellingham."

Jameson was ready. "Your honor, we wish at this time to request a writ of habeas corpus hearing in this matter."

The prosecutor began to argue, but then stopped, seeing the look the judge was giving him. The court adjourned, and Sarah was taken under guard back to the Bellingham Wing of Montgomery General, with a black ankle bracelet on her right foot.

Chapter Nine

Reynolds and Archer had pulled their chairs together to read the computer screen. The clerk that had brought the results in stood behind them. They read in silence for a moment before Archer turned around to the clerk.

"Do you think they could say it in English?" he asked.

Reynolds grunted and said, "It says they're two different people, just like the kid thought."

"In the summary section," the clerk said, pointing to the lower part of the screen. "14.2% chance they were written by the same individual," he said. "Margin of error 15.1%."

"And this'll hold up in court?" Archer asked.

"Oh, yes, this type of analysis is used all the time. Plagiarism cases, wills, libel, this laboratory has an excellent record."

"What's all this stuff here?" Reynolds asked, pointing to a table of numbers.

"Expected values, based on previous data analysis," the clerk read. "They show what they usually get, from samples of the same size."

"But these numbers are a lot smaller," Reynolds said. "It looks to me like they usually are a lot more certain of their conclusions."

The clerk read the numbers over his shoulder. "0.6% looks like the largest error," he said. "With confidences of 1.2%. I'm not sure that I know exactly what that means either."

"It means she's really good," Reynolds said. "We have years' worth of Wilson Bellingham's emails from before he was murdered. We have a much smaller sample of the emails that started to suddenly come from the grave, and while they are definitely different people, the new writer knows the old stuff by heart, and can mimic it so well that only the computer can tell it isn't him."

"She may be using a computer program to mimic his style and word choice," the clerk said.

"Wouldn't that make it a perfect match?" Archer asked.

The clerk shrugged. "You'd think so, wouldn't you? One computer is looking at it with one set of assumptions and the other is looking at it with a different set, maybe. Or maybe she didn't have all of the old emails."

"Or maybe she had a lot more than we do," Reynolds said. "We just used his emails. She might have his personal stuff -- old love letters, business reports, that kind of thing."

"But we got her," Archer said. "This is killer stuff for the prosecution. A few weeks after he suddenly stops sending out his emails, and people start asking questions, someone else starts sending out fake emails from the same computer he always used, with the same digital signature. That's a cover up."

"And we found her in possession of that computer," Reynolds said.

"Which we can't read," Archer replied. "So we can't actually prove it was the same computer."

"Not all wins are shut-outs," Reynolds said. "We have this bitch. She sent the emails from the same computer, with the same signature. Once the guys come back with the trace, we'll know that she sent them from Atlanta. That's the final nail."

A Distant Beacon

~

Sarah sat on the big couch in the recovery suite. Jameson sat next to her, and Doctor Williams stood by the large chair facing them. He was anxious to discuss her progress, but he gave Jameson deference, and Jameson wanted to talk about the legal situation, or at least that part he could discuss in front of the doctor.

"They'll have their own psychiatrists meeting with you after the 72 hour hold. They may try to extend that to 14 days. If we haven't been able to get a favorable bail decision by then, we might let them. You'll be getting to know this place pretty well. Let me know if there is anything you need, and I'll have it sent up from the house."

Sarah reached for his legal pad. "A new guitar," she said, "A Martin D-45 Dreadnought. They're keeping my old guitar as evidence. Maybe they think I hit someone with it. I'll need a computer, since they're also keeping that, although they won't be able to break the encryption. And a phone. And a piano, not a big one, there isn't room here, just something electric that will fit against the window."

"You're taking up music?" Jameson asked.

"Don't need to," Sarah said, glancing up at Williams. "Sarah Johnson plays guitar, Theresa Jennings plays piano, and Morganna Wilson draws and paints. That's the key to getting to their memories. Find the things they love."

Williams brightened. "So it's working," he said. "It's actually working!"

Sarah nodded. "We'll need to make some changes to the post-op notebook and the integration procedures, but yes, it seems to be a success. I still have some work to do on Morganna. It's hard to tell what is yet to uncover, and what is just hard to remember because it happened to a child so long ago."

A Distant Beacon

Jameson was interested in more immediate matters. "You *do* remember events just prior to the operation, is that correct?"

"I have all of Cordelia," Sarah said. "She loves business. The game of it, beating people at their own game, using money to keep score, manipulating people with it. She's kind of a bitch to most people; it's easy to see why she has such a small circle of friends. But once I let her handle business, she came right back and took over."

"The savant skills," Williams said. "It's part of the diagnosis for Wellman's. Each personality focuses on a particular skill to an obsessive extent. We didn't think to use that as a key to integration."

"We're going to need those memories," Jameson said. "I need to know all about Arthur Woods."

Sarah sighed. "We searched all over for other Wellman's cases, once Thomas found I was carrying the gene. It's rare, and since the personalities are usually fully functional, it is seldom that a case comes to light. Most carriers don't have the environmental triggers that bring on the breaks. But we found Woods by paying someone to scan FBI databases for Lockwood Act records."

"Highly illegal," Jameson said. "Genetic information in criminal records is supposed to be sealed."

"Yes," Sarah said. "That's one of our problems. Letting Woods be an issue in court might somehow cause that information to come out. Cordelia thought it was worth the risk."

"We needed a test subject," Williams said. "And he gave full informed consent."

"He was paid," Sarah said. "That's another ethical problem that could cost Thomas his ability to practice. Another thing we'll want to keep the court from discovering. The procedures all went as planned, but when he recovered, he was a blank. He had no recollection of his past life. There is no animal model for Wellman's, so a human subject was essential, and what we learned with Woods gave us a handle on how to prevent the loss of personality. We knew from functional studies of his brain just which areas to exercise, but we couldn't go back and work on Woods. It was too late. The exercises have to happen in the first weeks after the treatments."

She looked up at Williams. "What happened to Woods is all on me," she said. "I take full responsibility for that."

"But he gave full consent," Williams said.

"You can't consent to be murdered," Sarah said.

"That's a bit melodramatic," Williams argued. "It's not like we shot him or strangled him."

"Not *we*," Sarah said. "This is all on me. Cordelia made certain you had no real choice. As you said, it's her savant talent, and I won't let anyone else go down for this. It wouldn't be right."

"Wow," Jameson said. "This is going to be difficult. We won't know exactly what they've found out about Woods until the team has gone over the discovery file. Even then, we can't be sure they aren't holding something back, or won't find more in the meantime. Someone in the hospital is tipping them off. Do you have a list of everyone who knew anything about Woods?"

Williams leaned against the big chair. "I'll compile that for you. The surgical team, the gene therapy team, the nursing staff. However, we kept them all in the dark. None of them knew enough to put anything together. We treated it as a routine matter. The hospital does that kind of procedure six times a day. It's a normal treatment for a dozen types of dementia, only the gene

A Distant Beacon

therapy team would have a clue it was Wellman's we were treating, and that work was done in Austria, and they would have no way of telling who the patient was or where the treatment was taking place."

"We need to find the leak," Jameson said. "Someone knows or figured it out, and if we can find out who that is, we might have a better idea of how much they know, and whether we can make the witness look less credible."

"And damage some other perfectly innocent person," Sarah said. "God what a mess. Life was so easy for Cordelia. She had no heart. People were toys and tools. It's like everything that had hurt Morganna or Theresa was blocked off, so she was protected from ever feeling enough for someone to be hurt by them."

"It is very strange hearing you talk about yourself in the third person," Jameson said.

"Oh, I'm Cordelia," Sarah said. "But I'm also Morganna Wilson, and Theresa Jennings, and Sarah Johnson. I'm all of us. I can do what none of us can do. Michael, I fell in love. With someone I *knew* I couldn't trust. Someone who turned me in to the police. Someone who was trying to run a con on the rich tourist. I fell for him, completely. It hurts so much, but I would do it again in an instant. They couldn't have done that. They were all about walling off the ability to be hurt. You can't live a real life if you're too busy making sure you can never be hurt."

Tears were streaming down her face, and she reveled in them, the sign that she was a whole person. She leaned back on the couch and let them come.

"And God," she said, "If there is one person I would kill right now it would be Douglas Warwick." With that, she started giggling, and she couldn't stop. She put her arm around Jameson, and buried her face on his shoulder, wiping the tears on his suit, giggling. She slowly gathered her composure, but she still had an unshakeable grin on her face when she looked up at Williams and Jameson. "Pour Douglas," she said. "He tried so hard."

Jameson put his hand on her shoulder. "I really hope this side of you doesn't come out in court," he said. "Unless we really want you to spend the rest of your life in *this* place."

"This place isn't so bad," Sarah said. "I hear they grill up a mean rib-eye."

~

A Distant Beacon

The next morning, the uniformed guard at the door carefully inspected all of the items that had been delivered for Sarah. He gave up trying to open the electric piano to search for hidden weapons, but he shook the guitar and peered into the sound hole, using his flashlight. The tablet computer and phone he gave only cursory once-overs.

Doctor Williams came in a half hour later, to find her picking out an intricate arpeggio on the new guitar.

"Sarah's talent," he said, taking a seat on the couch and setting papers down onto the low table in front of him. "Before the court-ordered doctors get here, I'd like to go over the timeline, to see how well the integration has come along."

Sarah put down the guitar and joined him on the couch. "They have my notebook," she said. "So I'll have to do it all again, from memory."

Williams held a pad and pen in his hands. "What is the earliest thing you can remember?"

"That's hard. A lot of Morganna is out of sequence." She thought for a while. "Mom brushing my hair. Sandcastles at the beach. Swimming. I have no idea when those things happened, or in which order."

"How about birthdays?" Williams coached.

"Good idea." She paused. "Let's see, I remember seeing myself blowing out candles. Like a video, so that probably isn't a real memory, I mean a first-person memory. I remember my telescope, setting it up in the backyard to see sunspots, because I couldn't wait for it to get dark to see stars and the moon. I think that might have been Christmas though. I think my birthday is close to Christmas, so I can't tell which presents are birthday and which are holiday. Riding horses on the beach, that was a birthday. I was eleven. We were in Mexico; Dad had business, so I couldn't have a party with all my friends. Mom hated Mexico. She was scared. We went to the beach, there were horses, and she taught me how to ride. And I was really sore the next day."

Sarah noticed there were tears falling freely down her cheeks. "She was right to be afraid," she said. "They killed them both. Mom and Dad. Shot them and burned the boat. I can't see their faces. I could draw you a picture of each of the horses we rode that day in Mexico, and get every detail perfect, but Mom and Dad are just blanks. I was almost 17 years old. The guns, the fire, wetting my pants in the little skiff, waiting for it to get dark before I even let my head out from under the wet tarp. I was so cold. Rowing towards shore all night long. Blisters on my hands. Putting rocks in the skiff and tipping it over out past the breakers. Swimming back to shore in all my clothes. I can remember all of that, but I can't see their faces."

Williams was writing quickly. "You saw your parents get murdered? That is almost certainly the initiating trauma for the Wellman's dissociation."

"You think?" Sarah asked sarcastically. "My parents had set up safe houses all over the place. Drilled me on the addresses and the names we would assume at each one. They were terrified I would mess it up and give us all away. That's why I didn't end up like Woods every time I shifted. I had a ready-made identity that came complete with legal identification, a home, an income, the whole works. When Woods shifted, he had to start from nothing, so he took menial jobs and never got any higher education. Theresa Jennings finished high school and went to college. She almost got married."

Williams held the pad in one hand. The other hand had forgotten it was supposed to be taking notes. "Almost," he said.

A Distant Beacon

"He popped the question at a party at his mother's house, with all his friends and relatives there. They wanted her family to be at the wedding, and started asking questions about them that she couldn't answer. It was dangerous to have people asking questions about the past, about her parents, all that had to be forgotten or something terrible would happen. That's when Theresa shifted to Sarah Johnson, and left Atlanta to come out to Santa Barbara."

Williams was taking notes again. "The second shift was triggered by the memory of the initial trauma," he said. "That's classic Wellman's."

"The shift to Cordelia was six years later. The news was showing photos of two Mexican cartel leaders who had been decapitated in a gang war. I recognized them immediately. They were the ones who had killed Mom and Dad that night on *The Quest*. That's the name of our catamaran. We were going to sail around the world and forget about Dad's business with the Mexicans."

"So the memory of the men triggered the next shift," Williams said.

"Yes. Cordelia lived in Arizona. That was the first safe house Dad set up, and it didn't just have the normal stuff the others had. It had Dad's office and library. Correy fixated on Dad's journals, and read all his books. She became what he had become, a wiz at finance and investments. She also found all the rest of the money, where all the accounts were, but she couldn't get to them. They were under Dad's first alias."

"You called her Correy," Williams said.

"There are three people in the world who called Cordelia that. One was Cordelia herself. The others were Michael Jameson and Dick Ramsay. Those last two were part of the scheme to get Dad's money and start up Tygaard Securities."

Williams put the pen down, forgetting why he had it in his hand.

"Dad's name was Lee Wilson. He and his business partner Walter Bellingham had started a hedge fund called Wilson Bellingham. When Bellingham found out that their biggest client turned out to be a drug cartel, and that they were using him to launder money, he tried to turn them in and get out of doing business with them. They killed him. They came to Dad and told him our family would be next unless he concentrated the whole business on money laundering. Dad agreed."

Sarah leaned back on the couch and took a deep breath.

"The way Dad laundered the money involved squandering a lot of it on businesses that were failing. He would buy the business, and then customers from all over the world would suddenly start buying their products and services. With drug money, of course. The business would pay taxes, and look completely legal, and then they would sell it at a handsome profit and look like turnaround geniuses. Especially when the companies failed right after being under new management."

"Dad hated the cartel guys. He wanted out. However, he'd need a lot of money to stay safe. He started funneling the money into accounts that he had control of. To make that easy, he invented the person named Wilson Bellingham. That person could cash checks made out to the company of the same name. On the books it looked like a straightforward bank transfer, from one Wilson Bellingham account to another."

Williams appeared confused. "So Wilson Bellingham is your father?"

"Was. He's dead. Cordelia found Michael and Dick, two young lawyers whose ambitions were stronger than their sense of ethics. She hired an actor, and went to Las Vegas to get married to the

A Distant Beacon

actor, under the name Wilson Bellingham. The actor thought it was for a television commercial."

"And you had access to your father's accounts, as the wife of Wilson Bellingham," Williams said.

"Not just that," Sarah said. "His reputation as a turnaround expert and wizard investor. He came out of hiding, but only via email. The reclusive billionaire investor who was so paranoid he never let anyone see his face."

"Your father had stolen a billion dollars from the cartel?" Williams asked.

"Nowhere near it. It was a lot, however. The myth of vast wealth helped a lot in getting new money into the fund. Cordelia used a twist on Dad's original scheme. She still bought failing companies and spent a lot of money buying their products to make the stock go up. The leverage the fund provided made that easier. But she really was good at turnarounds, and once the companies had momentum, she would keep the ones that had really turned around, and sell the ones that hadn't. And once sold, suddenly no one was buying their products. The myth of the wizard Wilson Bellingham just grew more and more."

"So what's with all the police and the murder charges? You can just tell them there never was a Wilson Bellingham, and make it all go away!"

"And lose the whole company to lawsuits, and probably go to jail for fraud and stock manipulation, along with Michael Jameson and Judge Richard Ramsay. No, I have to figure out some other way to make the police back down. They obviously don't have a body. But they have someone who is spreading lies about a murder, and we can't counter that by telling the court we were lying about the supposed victim."

There was a knock on the door. They both rose from the couch, and Williams placed his notepad back into his briefcase and locked it. It was time to prepare for tomorrow's meeting with the prosecution's psychiatric team.

Chapter Ten

Detective Jonas Reynolds glanced at the computer screen and let out a low "Jesus Christ..." when he saw what had come up.

"Archer, get over here and check this out," he said.

David Archer rolled his chair over beside the taller man.

"This is what facial recognition came up with on those drawings we found in the Bellingham woman's room," he said.

"Santiago Garcia," Archer read, "And Ernesto Rodriguez, found decapitated outside of Nogales, Arizona. I remember that, the big drug war started right after that."

"She drew those pictures," Reynolds said. "Her charcoal fingerprints are all over the backs of them. There are no pictures of these guys anywhere on the Internet that show them looking like that, the mustache, the beard, the shirt collar. She drew those from memory."

"You think there's a connection somewhere," Archer said.

"Of course there is," Reynolds replied, irritated. "She drew these pictures. But look at this, what does that say to you?" He brought up two more screens.

"Cordelia Watson, Nogales, Arizona," Archer read. Then he studied the second screen. "Cordelia Watson weds Wilson Bellingham in civil ceremony in Cupid's Castle Wedding Chapel, Las Vegas, Nevada."

"Check the dates," Reynolds said.

"OK, so she was in Nogales when these dirt-bags lost their heads," Archer said.

"And she marries Bellingham a few months later. Well, who was the prime suspect in the Walter Bellingham murder case? That DEA file that came in?"

"The drug runners," Archer said.

"Based in Nogales, Mexico. Just across the border from where our psycho killer cuts the heads off of two drug lords to get revenge for her new fiancé, and starts a drug war."

"Christ on a crutch," Archer said.

"That's four murders now," said Reynolds. "This bitch has been a busy girl."

"That also explains why this Wilson Bellingham guy wouldn't let anyone see his face, or meet him in person. The Mexicans probably had a price on his head," Archer concluded.

"Maybe she decided it was time to collect," Reynolds said.

"So now we have motive," Archer said. "For three out of the four. Why did she off the Woods guy?"

"Maybe he knew something," Reynolds said.

"The guy shows up out of nowhere, no social security number, no job history, no prior address. Obviously a fake name. He's on the run from something. He hooks up with the wife of a billionaire, and then disappears. Yeah, he probably had something on her. Needed the money, on the lam for something, maybe drugs. Tries to blackmail our black widow. Not the brightest crayon in the box."

Archer leaned back in his chair. "Now we just have to prove it."

~

A Distant Beacon

At the soft, polite tapping on the door, Sarah got up to open it. Walter Hastings stood in the doorway, his neatly knotted tie just visible above the buttoned lab coat. She gestured him in.

"Welcome to my humble prison," she said.

"Is there really a policeman sitting outside your door?" Walter asked. "I couldn't tell. I'm pretty sure that hasn't happened on the Doctor Hathaway show, so I thought maybe he was real."

"Yes, that's Officer Perez," Sarah said. "It's probably OK if you call him Juan, but he doesn't seem to like it when I do. He thinks I might bite or something."

"Then I take it he hasn't read your chart," Walter said.

"Neither have you," Sarah said.

"Oh. I thought I had. I just couldn't remember if it was Morton's Neuroma or diabetic neuropathy." He was looking down at her feet.

"You were once a doctor weren't you?" Sarah asked.

"Podiatrist," he said. "Once a doctor, always a doctor. They can't take that away from you. But they took away my license after the accident."

"I imagine it might be difficult to practice in your condition," she said.

"Oh, I stay in pretty good shape. Two hours a day on the Stairmaster. Low impact, the joints will last longer." He saw the look on her face. "I know you meant my mental condition, I'm just playing with you."

"How is your treatment coming along?" Sarah asked.

"The pills seem to be working again," he said. "And Doctor Williams is teaching me lucid dreaming. I don't think that is helping at all."

"I thought lucid dreaming was your main problem," Sarah said.

"No, it's backwards from that. In lucid dreaming, your conscious mind knows it is unconscious, and controls the dream. My life is the opposite — the dream happens when I'm awake, and I can't tell what is real and what is a dream. So being able to change the dream would only help if the real part didn't change. Then I could tell if someone was real by putting a mustache on them. I tried imagining Nurse Alice without her clothes, and there she was, in the altogether, just doing her rounds like usual. I'm a bit happy I tried it on her instead of one of the male orderlies."

"But you knew she was real," Sarah said.

"Oh yes. It was time for our television show. We watch it together every day. So I knew she was supposed to be there, and there weren't two of her."

"And you knew she wasn't actually naked," Sarah said, grinning.

"Those things would never have fit in that bra she wears," Walter said. His grin sent them both into a fit of giggles.

"If I catch you staring," Sarah said, "I'll pinch you."

"And ruin all my fun?" Walter asked.

"I guess it's not the first time it's happened to me," Sarah said. "But I'm sure it happened a lot more when I was younger."

"I'll bet you broke a lot of hearts," Walter said.

Sarah studied his face, and thought of Douglas.

A Distant Beacon

"Well, this time it was my turn," she said.

Walter sensed the sudden change in the mood.

"Something happened while you were gone?" he asked.

"I fell in love," she said. "I keep telling myself it was just the whole integration thing, getting my emotions caught up with all of the alters. It was all so fast, you know? A couple of days together and I'm jumping on the poor guy. I should have known he was just after the money, I knew that from the beginning. I knew he was a con artist, I knew exactly what he was trying to do, and I fell into it anyway."

"I take it something happened, and it didn't end well?" Walter asked.

"He turned me in," she said. "I trust a crook and he turns me in to the police. So much for honor among thieves."

"You stole something?"

"No. They think I killed my husband. But he never existed, I made him up, so there was no one to kill. Then they found out about Artie, and that one really is all on me. That was my decision." She walked over to the piano and sat down on the bench, facing away from the keyboard. Her shoulders slumped.

"You were trying to help him," Walter said, walking over to sit in the chair facing her.

"And look what happened," she said.

They each sat, staring at the ground between them.

"So, you broke up with your new boyfriend because he turned you in to the cops," Walter said. "Why would he do that?"

"I don't know," Sarah said. "It doesn't make sense, does it? Correy beat him at the con game, and he was probably broke, but wouldn't he just try some new con? I think that's what we were all expecting. He had me, he could have just asked for the money and I'd have given it to him. When I saw him in the police car, he seemed so ashamed of himself. He wouldn't look at me."

"I'm not sure I followed any of that," Walter said. "So I know it was real. Why don't you call him and ask him why he did it?"

"We didn't use the phone," she said. "We used an email account; we shared the password and never actually sent the letters."

"How romantic," Walter said, grinning.

"It was cute," Sarah said. "Both sides being coy, nothing traceable. It was a communications channel we could trust. And when you're typing a message, you have more control than when you're blurting things out, or crying on a guy's shoulder."

"So you were vulnerable," he said.

"Total nutcase," she said. "Why do you think I'm here?"

"Well," Walter said, "there *is* that."

They both giggled again. It was a while before they could stop.

After dinner, when she was alone, lying on the big bed, she thought back on what Walter had said. Why hadn't she contacted Douglas? Besides the fact that they had taken her computer. She had one now.

However, she still didn't get up off the bed and find the tablet. Did she want to know? Was she afraid?

What if he had already tried to contact her? That got her off the bed. She found the tablet, and logged in to the shared email account.

There was a message from him. Several. She scrolled down to the earliest one and opened it.

"Leave town immediately," it said. "Cops grilled me, trying to find you. Guy from California, homicide detective. Talked a lot of trash about you. Gave him nothing, but you have to scram."

Sarah looked at the timestamp on the draft. It was the day she had not been able to find Douglas. The evening she had eaten alone in the hotel restaurant, waiting for him to show up. It had never occurred to her to use the email from the game to talk to him.

She read the other messages. The police had picked him up again, the next day, and kept him in the car as they canvassed all the hotels in the area, showing his picture to all the desk clerks. *He brought us right to you.* That's what they had meant.

She was crying again. Cordelia had never cried. Sarah never cried. Theresa and Morganna, on the other hand, were regular rain faces. She wiped the tears from her face. *Integrate*, she told herself. It's OK to cry, but don't let it take over.

She composed a message to Douglas. "Time to learn how to drive a stick shift," she typed. "I need you in Santa Barbara. The valet has the keys. Stay under the speed limit and don't get arrested. There's ten grand in an envelope under the spare. Stay in nice hotels, they'll take good care of the car."

She sent the email, and then called the hotel in Atlanta to let them know to give Douglas the keys.

She was locked in a mental hospital, with an electronic tracker on her ankle, a guard at her door, and a murder trial about to send her to jail and destroy her company and her friends. She could not remember ever feeling happier.

~

A Distant Beacon

The next morning, Sarah was busy.

"I need you to get all the information you can on Lee Wilson and Walter Bellingham," she said to the face on her phone. She gave the dates and addresses she knew. "Private investigators, any news organizations that reported on them, any public records, any relatives, whatever you can get. Charge it to me personally; this is not a Tygaard matter."

She closed the connection, and looked around the room. She had been sketching since very early in the morning, after finding an old photo of Lee Wilson in a web search. She had been hoping the sketches would bring back an actual memory of his face, but that had not happened. The tiny image of her father on the screen just did not have enough detail. It did not help that she had been up before dawn, doing research on the computer.

She showered and dressed, and was about to try sketching again when there was a knock at the door. Thomas Williams let himself in.

"I'm going to get a lock for that door," Sarah said to the doctor as he entered. "Something to teach you that a knock is a request, not a warning."

"I'm sorry," he said. "A hospital habit saves a lot of time." He did not sound like he was sorry at all. "I was wondering if you had been to breakfast yet."

"You came up seven flights to see if I was hungry?" she asked. "What's the real reason you're here?"

"Well, I have something to show you. It is down in the dining hall. I think you'll enjoy it." He wasn't usually this coy.

"Well, then," she said, putting her phone and computer in her purse, and walking towards the doctor and the door. "Is it something I'll have to unwrap?"

"No," he said, distracted by the drawings. "Who is this?"

"Dad, I think," Sarah said, opening the door. "I found a picture on the net, but it doesn't ring any bells. I thought drawing the face might help."

They walked to the elevator. "Did it?" Williams asked.

"Not a bit," she said. "The photo is so small, and they might have touched it up. Or it could be someone else entirely, mislabeled. The article was about Wilson Bellingham, the investment firm. But all it said was copied from their press release. Third quarter profits, all that stuff, nothing that would help."

The elevator stopped at the ground floor, and they walked into the dining room. Sarah saw Walter Hastings sitting at a table with another patient, but none of the other diners were familiar. It seemed to be the busy part of the morning shift.

"Try the special," Williams said, grinning, and handing her a menu.

Sarah read. The special was an Italian sausage omelet with marinara sauce. "OK," she said warily, "I guess I'll have the special."

"Me too," Williams said to the woman in the hairnet behind the counter. "And coffee, and a bran muffin."

"Just OJ, thanks," Sarah said.

"So, what's the surprise?" she asked.

"After breakfast," Williams said, grinning again. "You know what you said about using the savant talent to access the memories of the other alters? That was brilliant. In hindsight it seems so obvious, but I don't know if any of us here would have come up with that."

"I guess we're just lucky there was a piano in the hotel lobby," Sarah said slowly, suspicious of his small talk.

Throughout breakfast, Williams continued to avoid talking about why he had invited her down. He talked about her tricks of exploring around the edges of each alter's timeline, of finding the environmental triggers for the shifts, and of revisiting the traumas after the treatments.

When they had finished, he asked her slyly, "So, how did you like your omelet?"

She studied his face. "It was quite good," she said, wondering what was to come next.

"Then I think we should go pay our compliments to the chef," he said, rising from his seat.

Sarah followed him into the kitchen, where a muscular man in a white paper hat and white smock was expertly working an array of pans on a large industrial stove.

Sarah saw his face as he turned towards them. "Artie!" she almost screamed. She ran up to the man and grabbed his shoulders. "They told me you were dead!"

"Who told you that?" Williams asked, coming up behind her.

"The police!" she said. "That's one of the charges; they have me up for his murder."

"I never trusted cops much," Arthur Woods said, flipping an omelet.

"But you remember not trusting cops?" Sarah asked.

"It turns out Arthur is quite the short-order cook," Williams said. "You might even say it is a savant talent, in addition to the skills as a mechanic he had demonstrated when we first met."

"Doc wouldn't quit," Woods said. "He kept showing me pictures of different kinds of jobs and asking me what they were doing. I saw someone flipping a burger and something clicked."

Williams beamed. "He's made excellent progress. We've drawn up a timeline, and there's one more gap that we think might be related to carpentry."

"Something about making chairs," Woods said. "It just feels right."

Sarah's mind was racing. "This changes a lot," she said. "Can we keep this a secret for a while? Not mention to anyone that Artie is alive? It's something we can use, something to spring on them at the right moment."

"You're paying the bills, Mrs. B.," Woods said, grinning.

"Why would they think he was dead?" Williams wondered.

"When we know that, we might figure out who's been telling stories to the police," Sarah said.

She took her phone from her purse. "Jameson," she told it and waited for it to make the connection.

His face appeared on the screen. "We need to meet. You, me, the legal team, or at least the part of it we can fit in my living room."

A Distant Beacon

"You have the psych. eval. team meeting most of the day today," Jameson said. Sarah swore as he continued. "We could meet this evening, say six o'clock. What's up?"

"Nothing I want to say over the phone," she said. "But it's a game changer."

"We got our own surprise this morning," Jameson said. "They've added two names to the indictment." He looked down to read something. "Santiago Garcia and Ernesto Rodriguez," he said.

"Those names sound vaguely familiar," Sarah said, puzzled.

"They should," Jameson replied. "You've been drawing their faces in charcoal."

"The guys who killed my parents," Sarah said. "What have they got to do with my case?"

"They're claiming you killed them. And left their heads on a fence in Nogales."

Sarah felt cold. "If anyone deserved that, it would be those two," she said.

"That's not something I think you should repeat," Jameson said. "They say they have motive, but they aren't saying what it is yet. Let's not give them one."

He was brushing it off, but Sarah was not so sure. She tried to remember what she had been doing around that time. Had she had one of her blackouts? She couldn't remember.

"Their heads on a fence," she repeated.

"Yeah," Jameson said. "Pretty gruesome. It sounds like a hit, someone wanted to send a message. Cartel internal squabble. It erupted into a full-scale war."

"Is that what the report says?" Sarah asked.

"I don't know, we'll be getting copies later," Jameson said.

"I'd like to see those," she said.

"You sure?" Jameson sounded doubtful.

"Yeah," she said. "Closure, I think."

"OK, I'll make sure you get them."

"Thanks," Sarah said, somewhat distantly.

"See you at six then," Jameson said.

"At six," Sarah said, and disconnected.

Williams checked his watch. "We should probably get you to the meeting room," he said.

Sarah looked up at him, and then at the big man at the stove. "Artie, you have no idea how good it is to see you," she said.

The big man smiled, and flipped another omelet, deftly tossing the pan in one hand.

"And breakfast was wonderful," she said, grinning back.

On the way to the elevator, she considered how she wanted to deal with the team of psychiatrists from the court. She had starting to feel in control again, and that might not be the best face to show them.

Chapter Eleven

The meeting room was huge, with one wall made all of glass, facing the view of the ocean and the cliffs below. Sarah could see gulls gliding on the updraft at the edge of the cliff. She watched them as four men she did not know organized their papers on the long conference table. They clustered in the middle of the big table, leaving Sarah and Williams on the other side, facing the window.

A fifth man was setting up a video camera aimed at Sarah's face. She looked at the blinking red light for a moment, and considered making a face, but thought better of it a moment later. She put on a congenial smile and watched the four men get prepared. It was getting late in the morning, and Sarah was already wondering how soon they were going to break for lunch.

"I think we can get started," said the man nearest the cameraman. "I am Doctor Albert Czerny. To my left are doctors Peter Bergman, Randolph Thompson, and Gerald Morgenstern. We are here today for the psychological evaluation of Mrs. Cordelia Bellingham."

Sarah smiled into the camera and nodded to it.

Czerny continued. "I'd like to start with some routine simple questions. Mrs. Bellingham, do you know the date today?"

"I do," she said.

"Could you please state it for the record?"

"August fourth," she said.

"What did you do last Christmas?" he asked.

"Can I ask what relevance that question has to all of this?" Sarah asked, waving at the four men.

"These are routine questions. This one in particular tells us about your memory."

"My memory has many holes in it," Sarah said. "That is normal for someone with my diagnosis. I have Wellman's Identity Disorder. I have been here at Montgomery General being treated for it for some time now."

The men at the table murmured to one another for a minute or two. Peter Bergman was the first to speak. "We are not familiar with that disorder," he said. "Who performed the diagnosis?"

"I did," Williams said, and the camera panned over to him. "Wellman's is a genetic disorder, quite rare. We have identified six individuals with the genotype, and two with the disorder itself. One is Cordelia Bellingham, and the other is Arthur Woods. Not all carriers of the trait have the disorder. There is an environmental component that is required."

One of the doctors was showing the others an image on a tablet. Czerny looked at the tablet, and then continued. "We'll look into the disorder when we break for lunch. In the meantime, could we get back to the questions? Mrs. Bellingham, what did you do last Christmas?"

"I was in Peru," she said. "The Tygaard Foundation supports an orphanage there, and we were distributing gifts to the children."

"Next question," Czerny said. "What makes you happy?"

Sarah thought for a moment. "I get satisfaction from accomplishing things," she said.

"The question was 'What makes you happy?'," Czerny said.

She looked at him, and then at the other three doctors, and thought about the night before. "Learning that someone you loved isn't an untrustworthy jerk after all," she said. She grinned broadly.

More murmuring among the four doctors.

"Do you have mood swings, depression, or manic episodes?" Czerny asked.

"No," she said. Then she amended that. "When I connect with another of my personalities, that is usually quite emotional. That would look like a mood swing, I guess, but it's just adjusting to someone else's mood."

This brought more discussion. Williams rested his hand on her knee briefly, under the table. She put her hand on his, and squeezed it in recognition.

"Are you currently taking any drugs?" Czerny asked.

"No," she said.

"Have you taken any drugs, prescription or otherwise, for recreational use?" he asked.

"No. I like to keep my head clear," she said. "There's enough rattling around in there without adding garbage."

"Will you submit to blood tests for drugs and hormone levels?" he asked.

"I will," she said. "You can also see the results of all of the tests performed during my treatment. That should keep you busy; I've been quite the pincushion here."

"Have you ever felt suicidal, or had thoughts of suicide?" Czerny asked.

"Yes," Sarah said. "Several years ago. Theresa woke up at Cordelia's house, and thought she could drown herself in the pool. She didn't know Morganna was an excellent swimmer."

More murmuring. "I'm sorry," Czerny said. "I'm having some trouble making sense of that last statement."

"Theresa Jennings is the alternate personality in control while I was in college and grad school. Cordelia Bellingham is the personality in control for most of the last seven years. I was born Morganna Wilson, and the Wellman's symptoms first showed up when I was 17, and watched my parents being murdered."

The four doctors were silent for several seconds. Then they began discussing this new information among themselves.

Morgenstern was the first to speak up. "I think we're getting somewhere. Your parents were murdered, you say, in front of you, and you once attempted suicide. Are the two events related to one another?"

"Other than that they both happened to *me*?" Sarah asked. "I don't think so. Theresa never knew about Morganna's parents."

"But what happened to your parents is what set off your condition? The multiple personalities?" Czerny chimed in.

"That's the current theory," Sarah said. "Wellman's is rare, and there just aren't a lot of cases to study. Since not all carriers come down with symptoms, there is presumably an environmental trigger."

Randolph Thompson may have been feeling a little left out. "Which personality is in control at this time?" he asked.

Sarah considered this. "Pretty much all of them," she said. "The treatments are working, and the Wellman's seems to be under control, and may be cured. There are bits of Morganna that are still missing; she's the hardest to get in touch with. It's like she's shy, watching all of us find each other."

"And just what is the nature of these treatments?" Czerny wanted to know.

"I'm afraid that is proprietary information at this point," Williams said, before Sarah could respond. "Pre-publication, and there are patents involved."

None of the doctors on the other side of the table liked this. There was more murmuring. Morgenstern changed the subject. "Your parents were murdered while you watched. Can you tell us more about that?"

"My father was in the business of laundering money for the Del Rio cartel in Nogales, Mexico. He quit, and they found him and killed him. And my mother."

"And you watched this?" he pressed.

"I did," she said.

"And what was your reaction?" he continued.

Sarah was getting annoyed. "I kept my mouth shut and wet my pants," she said. "What would you have done?"

"But you saw who did it?" he asked.

"I did," she said.

"If you saw them again, what would you do?" Morgenstern asked, not deterred by her tone of voice.

"Are they armed?" she asked.

"Yes," Morgenstern said, hesitatingly.

"Are they shooting?" she asked.

"Yes," he said, a little more confidently.

"I'd seek cover and return fire," she said.

"Where did you get your firearm?" Morgenstern asked.

"Where did they get theirs?" Sarah asked exasperatedly, throwing her arms wide in an appeal to the four doctors across the table.

Czerny intervened. "I think we're covered this area in enough detail," he said. "I'd like to talk about your husband, Wilson Bellingham."

"I'm all ears," Sarah said.

Czerny looked puzzled for a moment. "I meant we'd like to hear about your husband," he corrected.

"I'll bet you would," Sarah said. "Along with half of Wall Street and most of the news organizations in the country."

There was silence from the other side of the table. Sarah waited.

"How would you describe your marriage?" Czerny finally asked.

"I don't," Sarah said.

"Was there trouble between the two of you?" he asked.

"No," she said.

"Was he abusive?" he continued.

"Not at all," she said.

A Distant Beacon

"Were there any money problems?" he continued, and then added quickly, "Were there any problems of a sexual nature?"

"No, and no," Sarah said.

"If I may," Bergman interrupted, "I'd like to pursue the matter of the alternate personalities," he said. "You mentioned four, I believe."

"Three," Sarah corrected, "Plus Morganna."

"And they were unaware of one another," he said.

"At first," Sarah said. "Then Theresa left a note for Cordelia, after the incident in the pool. So, Cordelia knew about Theresa, and started looking for help. After a few years of research, she found Doctor Williams here, and they started planning the treatment."

As she spoke, Sarah grew uncertain. The three alters did not know about one another. But what about Morganna?

Her thoughts were interrupted by more questions.

"Do any of these personalities act on impulse?" Morgenstern wanted to know.

"What do you mean?" Sarah asked.

"Do they always think things through, or are they subject to impulses or urges?" he clarified.

Sarah thought about how Peter Thompson had been sure Cordelia could get away with murder.

"Cordelia liked to be in control," Sarah said. "She planned everything. The others, not so much, but no urges or impulses."

"Did they always know right from wrong?" Morgenstern asked.

"Do you?" she replied.

There was a silence. Morgenstern let it go. "Are you an introvert or an extrovert?" he asked.

Sarah didn't know. "Is there something in between?" she asked.

Morgenstern ignored her answer. "Are you ever hostile, or aggressive?" he wanted to know.

"I'm getting there," Sarah said.

Williams stood up. "I think this might be a good time for a break," he said. The doctors on the other side of the table glanced up at him, and Czerny looked like he was about to object, but checked his watch instead.

"I think we can break for lunch," he said, and stood up. He reached his hand across the table towards Williams, who shook it distractedly as he watched Sarah leave the room. He nodded to the group, and followed her out the door, leaving the doctors to find their own way to the dining hall.

He caught up with her on the way to the elevator.

"What do you think?" he asked.

"Those clowns haven't a clue," Sarah said. "I almost let Cordelia loose on them; they wouldn't have stood a chance."

"But you didn't," he said.

"What would have been the point? They are either going to stand up in court and declare me nuts, or they are going to say I'm sane and can go to jail. In either case, we just buy a bunch of shrinks to say the opposite, if that suits our plans. Letting Cordelia count coup would just be a waste of time." She pushed the button on the elevator to go up.

A Distant Beacon

"Then why do you seem upset?" Williams asked.

"It's something about Morganna," Sarah said. "Something I have to work out. There are all these holes in the timeline. Times when the alters lose days, but no other alter remembers. It has to be Morganna, but I can't reach her. Drawing doesn't cut it, there has to be some other way to get to her."

"The art isn't her obsession, then?" Williams asked. "Wellman's subjects have their savant talents because they obsess. Maybe the artistic skill is just ordinary artistic skill."

"You see where I'm going, right?" Sarah asked.

"You think she might be obsessed with the murder," he said.

"That's what I'm going to try," she said. "If it had happened to you, wouldn't you obsess a little?"

"I think obsessing a little might be an oxymoron," he said.

The elevator doors opened, and Sarah entered. She watched the doors close on William's face. He seemed deep in thought.

~

Back in her room, Sarah called Jameson.

"You said they were adding the two Mexicans to the list," she said. "Did anything about them get added to the discovery brief?"

Jameson looked away from the phone for a moment, and moved some papers around on his desk.

"There are some police reports," he said. "And copies of DEA and FBI files."

"Send them up to me, could you?" she said. "I want to check into all aspects of my parents' murder. That includes everything about how the killers got their own numbers punched. Do we have anyone we can spare to look into my parents?"

"Researchers and private detectives can be hired at any time," Jameson said. "All it takes is money. I'll have Elaine set it up."

"Thanks," Sarah said. "See you at six."

"At six," he said. The screen went dark.

She had a roast beef sandwich sent up to her room, and started making a timeline of all the unexplained gaps in her memories. She could not find any particular triggers for them. Unlike the other shifts, these seemed random.

You were up to something, Morganna. What was it?

Sarah went back to the murder of her parents. If Morganna were obsessed with that, then Sarah would obsess over that as well. When had it taken place? She remembered the cold. Was that the actual air temperature, or the cold of the water? How old was she when it happened? Sixteen or seventeen. Birthday. She was seventeen. Her birthday had been a trip to St. John's, sailing that little sloop with the shallow keel, snorkeling in the coral, just

A Distant Beacon

mom, dad, and the birthday girl. Always moving around, never having any close friends.

The big catamaran was much later. September off the California coast. Good winds, making good time. Heading north on a beam reach. She counted back to get the year.

All right, now what were Theresa's earliest memories? School. Atlanta. First day in college. Confident, know-it-all. Helping a girl with her schedule. She could not recall registering for school, or picking her classes. Just starting school. The add/drop deadline for classes was a week away, and she didn't know whether to keep the calculus class.

She used the computer to look up the deadlines for classes. November 29th. Her earliest memories as Theresa were just a week before, say the 22nd. What remained of September, all of October, and the first three quarters of November were lost. Someone had enrolled her in school. Who?

After lunch, the meeting resumed downstairs. The four psychiatrists had used their time to learn about Wellman's, and Sarah was thankful that most of their time was spent questioning Williams instead of her. She half listened as she went back over the details of the memory gap, trying to peel back the edges. *Obsess with the murder.* What would a seventeen-year-old girl do after someone killed her parents? Where would she go?

She was still lost in thought when everyone else in the room began to stand up. The meeting was over, and she rose from her chair feeling tired. A lot had happened already today, and the meeting with Jameson was still to come.

"You were pretty quiet in there," Williams said, as they walked to the dining hall.

"Thanks for deflecting all that for me," she said.

"Did something happen during lunch?" he asked.

"I'm just trying to work out the timeline. I'm missing a couple months after they killed my family. Before I started college. That's got to be important. But there is nothing there. It's like Morganna is hiding it from me."

"Why do you say that? You've had lots of memory lapses."

She shook her head. "This is different somehow. It feels purposeful in some way. I don't know. It's just a feeling. I could be way off track."

"You have all the others," Williams said. "There is just this one holdout. Of *course* it would feel like she was hiding from you. We all attribute movements in the grass to tigers when it's just the wind. We're the result of millions of years of survivors, and the ones who thought 'tiger' when it was wind outlived the ones who thought 'wind' when it was tiger."

"There are a bunch of holes in my memories," Sarah said. "Not just stuff I can't remember, but times when one of us woke up and found out we were missing hours or days from our lives. The shifts between the alters were different. Except for Theresa waking up to kill herself, they were all permanent. And they all had obvious triggers. These little vacations are different. There is no trigger. And life just goes on for the alter that was there before."

"And you think these were all reversions back to Morganna," he said.

"There are no other alters, I'm pretty sure of that," she said.

"And why do you think these were purposeful, that she is hiding from you?"

A Distant Beacon

"Because there is never any spillover. When Sarah woke up in Atlanta, she made a mess of Theresa's life. When Theresa woke up in Cordelia's house, she left a note. When I woke up in the recovery room, I almost messed up all of Cordelia's plans. But all of these little breaks, there's no spillover. She leaves a painting behind, and none of the alters think that's strange. No one in their lives asks them about what she has been doing. There's no room full of paints and an easel."

Sarah had a realization. "It's like Morganna knew all about the alters, and could fit right in. She knew how to slip into their lives without making waves. Like she'd been watching the alters all along. Her own little soap opera."

They reached the dining hall. Walter Hastings waved them over to his table.

"Mr. Woods made tacos for lunch," he said. "He's quite versatile. A big improvement."

"I thought the food was pretty good," Sarah said. "Even before he started working in the kitchen."

"But never tacos," Walter said. "He put flour tortillas around the crisp corn tortillas, so you could eat them without making a mess. I'd never seen them done that way before."

"He is definitely talented," Williams agreed.

"Speak of the devil," Sarah said, as Arthur Woods joined them at the table.

"I'm glad they give you some time off," Williams said.

"It's therapy, doc. It brings back things. Not all of it fun or pretty, but it's nice to have," Woods said.

"Tell me," Sarah said. "Do you have the early memories yet? Before your first shift?"

"That was the easiest," Woods said. "Nothing weird happened until I was nineteen. Signed up for boot camp after high school, and then wham! I was someone else, getting odd jobs at fast food places."

"Was there a gap in between?" she asked.

He thought for a moment. "I don't think so. I remember hitchhiking from the recruiter's place, without knowing why I had been there. Or caring. It was like walking out the door flipped a switch, and I was a new person."

"Not me," Sarah said. "I have these gaps I can't reach."

"The doc'll get you through. He's great," Woods said.

"Yes," Sarah said, looking over at Williams. "He certainly is."

"So these people we're going to meet," Woods said. "They friends of yours?"

"My lawyers," Sarah said. "But yes, at least one of them is a good friend. Michael Jameson. He's a little business-like for most people, but he grows on you."

"Which one of us needs a lawyer?" Woods asked. "You, or me?"

She laughed. "Me. You are in the clear. And the solution to one of my problems. The police think I killed you."

Woods was amused by this. "What is it that the Huckleberry Finn guy said? Someone was exaggerating?"

A Distant Beacon

"Here's the thing," Sarah said. "I want to spring you on the court all of a sudden, out of the blue. So no one but my team should know you were never dead."

Woods grinned. "You make it sound like a zombie movie," he said.

"I just want you to keep a low profile for a couple days," Sarah said. "Can you do that?"

"If someone asks me who I am, I can say Jimmy Stevenson," he said.

"Was that your name when you were a kid?" Sarah asked.

He nodded. "Maybe I should go by Jim though," he said. "Or maybe James."

They selected their dinners, and Woods examined each one when they were ready, looking for anything he could learn about cooking. He politely refrained from any criticism, saying he was sure the regular chef had lots to teach him.

After dinner, Sarah, Williams, and Woods went back to the big meeting room to wait for Jameson.

When the legal team arrived, Sarah introduced them.

"Gentlemen," she said, "Meet Arthur Woods."

There was silence for a moment. Jameson was the first to recover. "You seem remarkably well for a dead man," he said, reaching out to shake Woods' hand.

"I keep in shape," Woods said, gripping the lawyer's hand firmly in proof.

"This *does* change things," Jameson said. "We can drop one charge immediately."

"Actually," Sarah said, "I was thinking it might be better to spring all of our surprises at once."

Jameson raised an eyebrow. "We have more surprises?" he asked.

"There's always hope," Sarah said. "What have you folks been working on?" She waved Williams and Woods out the door. They had served their purpose, and it was time to get to work.

"The emails," Jameson said. "They had a service look at all of Wilson Bellingham's public emails, and they compared them to his emails that were sent while you were in Atlanta. The results say that they were sent by two different people. We don't have an answer to that. We're looking at ways to discredit the analysis, or the firm, or the collected data."

Sarah pulled the papers that Jameson was referring to over so she could read them. "Can we use the same firm for our own analysis?" she asked.

"Sure," Jameson said, uncertainly. "To help discredit them?"

"Maybe," she said. "We know the same person wrote the emails. But it looks like a different person did. What if we show that Cordelia Bellingham's emails before and after Atlanta also show the same effect? That Cordelia is now a different person?"

"They'll want to see all of those emails," Jameson said. "That could cause problems. Give them ammunition for something."

"We'll stick to the public emails," Sarah said, "Like they did for Wilson. Letters to news organizations, charities, employees, that kind of stuff. No private business correspondence. Nothing about the case."

A Distant Beacon

"What if it says she's the same person?" Jameson asked.

"Then we'll know there is a flaw in the analysis, and we can look for it," Sarah replied. "But it won't. I'm not Cordelia Bellingham anymore." She paused in thought. "What else have you got?"

"The DEA files, the FBI files, and the police reports on the deaths of Lee Wilson and Walter Bellingham."

He slid the folders over to Sarah. She opened the DEA report on the beheadings first. She began reading, but something was bothering her, making it hard to concentrate on the text. She went back to start over, but her eyes locked on the name of the DEA agent at the top of the page.

"What do we know about this person?" she asked, pointing to the name. "I know that name from somewhere."

"Timothy Muller," Jameson read. "Doesn't ring any bells. Someone do a search in our files," he said, looking at one of the other lawyers. The other man began pecking at his computer.

"I think I've met him," Sarah said. "I can almost picture his face. I just can't place where or when."

"Not coming up," the lawyer at the computer said. "I'll run a profile on him."

Sarah read the report. As she scanned the grisly details of the deaths of the two men, something inside her was pleased. These men had killed her family, and changed her life forever. She felt pride, as if she had killed them herself.

She closed the folder. "I'll study these later," she said. "For now, let's talk about how to inform the court that Wilson Bellingham never existed, without causing further damage to all involved. I think it's clear we can't go on pretending he's hiding somewhere."

"That could be tricky," Jameson said.

"I have a plan," Sarah replied. "And I have someone working on it as we speak. We start a whisper campaign on the stock. We leak that the real brains behind Tygaard is Cordelia, and that no one can show Wilson Bellingham ever existed. We make it look like a stock play. We make sure the stock jumps on the news, using our normal methods. Then we show the source is a known stock manipulator. Create uncertainty."

"The burden of proof is on the prosecution," Jameson said. "They will have to prove he exists, or existed, and you can plead the fifth."

"That's the other surprise," Sarah said.

"Risky," Jameson said. The other lawyers seemed to agree.

"You guys work on Plan B then," Sarah said. "And maybe C, too. This part I can handle."

"It *is* rather classic Cordelia Bellingham," Jameson agreed, grinning.

~

A Distant Beacon

That evening, Sarah pored over the reports. *Obsess about it. Try to reach her.* The catamaran had never been found, although burned bits of things were found on the shore after the body of Lee Wilson was discovered. Clarice Wilson's body was never found.

Walter Bellingham had been found in his home. He'd been shot twice in the chest, and once in the head. The door to his house had been broken open, and nothing in the house was missing. The gun had been wiped clean and left next to the body. The DEA report outlined what Bellingham had reported about the use of the firm to launder money.

If the DEA knew that Wilson Bellingham was being used by the cartel, why did they let dad continue?

She put down the report and closed her eyes, leaning back in her chair. Timothy Muller. The face in her mind would not focus. She had met him, she knew that. *Morganna knows him.*

Sarah got out the charcoal pencils and the sketchpad, and began drawing. At first, a generic face. Then, gradually, details. The jawbones. The cheeks. The hairline. Bit by bit, the sketch took shape, until she was looking at the man she was sure was Timothy Muller. She stared at the face, but no more recognition came.

She glanced at the clock on the computer screen and put away the sketch. Douglas Warwick should be somewhere halfway to California by now. She hoped he was not still driving this late. She picked up the tablet and dialed the number on the business card he had given her when they first met. His face appeared on the screen.

"Hey there," she said.

"Hey yourself," he replied.

"Enjoying your trip?"

"Getting the hang of the stick shift. But it's mostly highway driving, and like you said, it can do everything in fifth or sixth gear if I forget." He seemed to be leaning against pillows on a bed.

"I'll be glad to see you," she said.

"Not just the car?" he asked, smiling.

"No, you can *have* the car. I want you. But I also have a job for you, something you are uniquely qualified for."

"You're giving me the car," he echoed.

"Just like a man," she said. "You spill your heart, say *I want you*, and he only hears about the car."

"I want you too," he said. "Really, I do. But that's quite a car."

"Next time I see you, you'd better have roses," she said. "You're really not good at this romance thing."

"That wasn't really your sister, was it?" he asked softly, changing the subject.

"No, that was me," she said.

"So, what the police said, about..." he stopped.

"My condition," she finished for him. "I have something called Wellman's Identity Disorder. It's not schizophrenia, but there are multiple personalities. It's a genetic disorder. But my doctor has come up with a cure. I'm getting better every day."

He was silent for a while. She watched his face on the screen. "You know that doesn't matter to me," he said.

"It should," she said. "You should know."

A Distant Beacon

"And you told me. And we can talk about it. But it doesn't change how I feel about you."

"That's sweet," she said. "And it makes me happy." Then she grinned broadly. "But you'd better not forget the roses."

He laughed, and she laughed with him. "I miss you," she said.

"Me too," he replied. "But I should be there by tomorrow night."

"No speeding," she said.

"Oh come on," he said. "Some of those highways are just wide open. And all the traffic is doing eighty at least."

"Eighty isn't speeding," she said. "That car can do over two hundred. But trying anything close to that is suicide if you haven't trained with the car. I want you here in one piece. And if you get caught in that car doing ninety or more, they'll put you behind bars."

"I'll be good," he said. "But I'll still be there sometime tomorrow night. Early start and all that."

"Don't drive sleepy," she said.

"Yes, mother," he laughed. "So what's this job?"

"A whisper campaign," she said. "Saying that Wilson Bellingham never existed, and that Cordelia Bellingham did it all herself."

"No one's going to buy that," he said.

"How did I fall for such a sexist?" she asked. "Why wouldn't they?"

"He's a legend," he said.

"Exactly. A myth. Never existed."

"You're serious," he said.

"Dead serious," she said.

"You don't mean..."

"No, he's not dead, you dolt. He never existed."

"You built Tygaard all by yourself?"

"I had a whole team of people helping. But it was my team. The name Wilson Bellingham was just a convenience."

"Jesus," he said. "So the whisper campaign..."

"Is to keep me out of jail. You can't kill someone who never existed."

"So you didn't..."

"No, I didn't kill him. You were coming all this way to be with the girl you thought was crazy and killed her husband?"

"Well, not, no, I mean..."

"I'm just messing with you," she said. "But I *did* build Tygaard, and there never was a Wilson Bellingham, and I'm getting better every day with my treatments."

"And I'm uniquely qualified..."

"Yes. I knew all about you from the moment I saw you take my wallet from my bag."

"You saw that," he said.

"The whole wall was a mirror," she said.

"And you played me," he said.

A Distant Beacon

"Hey, what can I say? You're such a cutie, I couldn't resist."

"I lost over a hundred grand," he said.

"I said you can keep the car," she replied. "And anyway, this new job pays really well."

"It does, does it?"

"And there are fringe benefits," she said coyly.

"I'm looking forward to those," he said, his voice now soft and low.

"Get some sleep," she said. "You have a long trip in the morning."

"You take all the fun out of phone sex," he said.

"See you tomorrow night," she grinned.

"With roses," he said.

She winked, and disconnected.

The sketchbook was on the table as she set down the tablet, and she could not resist opening it and looking again at Timothy Muller. He was important. Where and when had Morganna met him? Somehow, he was the key to why she still felt she had done something unspeakably evil.

~

In her dream, Timothy Muller's face kept changing. Sometimes he had a beard, sometimes not. Sometimes he had long hair, sometimes short. When he was talking to her father, he had no touches of gray. When he was sitting across the table from her at a small cafe, his beard and sideburns were ash and white.

"You can't just walk in anytime you like," he was saying. "Someone might recognize you, or ask questions. We need a protocol, like the one we set up for Lee. Ways we can communicate by phone or electronically, and guarantee some security. Ways to indicate whether you are alone or being watched. Ways to alert us when you are in danger that don't give you away."

She remembered. Placing ads online offering to trade Civil War cannons for live Arctic foxes. Calling for Reginald Helmsworthy, or Zachary Nahtscurry. Sending specific amounts of money to flagged bank accounts as a code.

She also remembered being chastised for anonymously posting bank account statements to public anti narco-trafficking blogs in Mexico, and to Mexican newspapers. Statements that proved someone was embezzling from the Del Rio cartel. Bank accounts owned by Santiago Garcia and Ernesto Rodriguez. She felt a warm glow from seeing the results. It was time to move on.

"Now we have to start over from scratch," Muller was saying. "We had informants in the Del Rio. They are all dead. Three new organizations are forming from the remains of Del Rio, and we have no one inside."

"That's because you're looking in the wrong places," she had said. "I have people on the inside. And there are five organizations, not three. If you can arrange safe passage for the children, I can deliver. A full ride for the families, and they will be your eyes and ears."

A Distant Beacon

"I can't offer the deal you had," he said.

"They aren't asking for that. They just want their families to be safe. I can't do that alone."

"You've done enough, Anna," he said. "It's time to let it go."

She woke with tears falling freely down her face. It was early, and the sun had yet to brighten the sky through the window, but she quickly got out of bed and reached for the sketchpad. The faces of her parents quickly took form on the pad, although the tears made it difficult to see.

Chapter Twelve

After she showered all the charcoal from her hands and face, dressed, and ordered breakfast, she placed an ad online, offering to trade Turkish cigarettes for Moroccan sandals. She was finishing breakfast when the ad got a reply. *Can you ship to New Mexico?*

Sorry, you'll have to pick them up in person. Ask at the desk.

She thought about the first time she had seen Timothy Muller. He had come out to the docks to talk to her father. She had just come in from sailing and the salt and sun had made her skin itch, but she didn't want to scratch in front of the stranger. She remembered how he stopped talking whenever she entered the room, and then tried to convert to small talk. The Mexicans were much better at this than he was. She left to take a shower.

She remembered the other times, when his secret was out in the open. She remembered coming to him, three days after her parents were killed, and travelling by bus and taxi in the same clothes she had worn to swim ashore. Terrified and angry, telling him what she had seen. Asking him to teach her how to shoot a gun.

The newspaper that had come with breakfast made her smile. In the business section was an article asking if Wilson Bellingham had ever really existed. It cited a study comparing the emails of Cordelia Bellingham to Wilson Bellingham, and concluding that one person had written all of them, up until his disappearance, after which another person began writing emails as both people.

She put away the paper and went down to the meeting room to await the second day of her psychiatric evaluation.

The doctors, when they arrived, were much better informed about Wellman's Identity Disorder. They asked her and Williams questions to clear up inconsistencies, but they seemed to accept the diagnosis. The rest of the morning was spent with Sarah filling out written tests, MPI, CPI, IQ, and similar evaluations. She was happy to be alone with the papers, and not dealing with adversarial psychiatrists.

During the break for lunch, she met with Jameson and the legal team.

"We've received notice from the DEA that they want to participate in any ongoing hearings," he said. "Did you contact them? No one on our team has."

"I made contact with Timothy Muller," she said. "Not by phone, so I can't be sure it actually got to him specifically. But I am glad we now have their attention."

"They are asking for a closed hearing," Jameson said. "Demanding, actually. They want the records sealed."

"I know why they would want that," Sarah said. "But I think it's best if I let them tell you what they want you to know, rather than filling you in myself. Is that going to cause a problem for the team?"

Jameson and the legal team looked at one another. They didn't appear happy, but shrugs and nods indicated they would not press the matter.

"I can guess that it has something to do with the two new charges," Jameson said. "We'll wait for the DEA to fill us in on that. On the first charge, I saw the news this morning," he said, nodding to Sarah. "It seems we're trying to kill two birds with one stone. Create doubt that there was a victim at all, and attack their theory about a different person writing the new emails. I hope that confusion doesn't backfire on us. And of course we have Mr. Woods to take care of the second charge."

The lead lawyer spoke up. "Creating doubt about Wilson Bellingham may help us in the trial itself, but it won't be enough to ensure bail in the meantime. They still have witnesses and evidence that under the Harding Act are enough to hold Mrs. Bellingham for trial."

"If we can make the prosecution look bad enough at the hearing," Sarah said, "they may decide to cut their losses and drop the charges."

"A high profile case is what prosecutors dream about," the lead lawyer said. "Especially as elections near."

"That cuts both ways," Sarah said. "But we should continue on both fronts. The team should work as they see best, and I will continue trying to get this whole thing nipped in the bud. Dick Ramsay is still in a position to make choices, and I'd like to give him only one by the time the hearing takes place, and I hope to make that one an easy one for him."

"Just keep us in the loop this time," Jameson said. "Surprises are not efficient. We may be working on something that you completely undermine or make irrelevant, and that time is lost forever."

Sarah looked at the group. "I'm sorry. I'll try to be more transparent. However, the DEA information really should come from them. I'll be working on making Wilson look like a myth, and take the credit for Tygaard, as long as the market seems to like the idea. If the stock takes a hit, however, I may back out of that completely."

A Distant Beacon

It was time to get back to the doctors in the meeting room, and Sarah was almost happy at the thought. She didn't like making Jameson upset with her. He had his own neck to protect in all of this, and she had to keep some cards close to her chest.

The doctors had scored the tests. They had also compared them to the tests Williams had provided, that Cordelia Bellingham had completed before her treatment. There was quite a bit of disagreement over how to interpret the results.

"It is clear that she is test savvy," Czerny was saying, ignoring Sarah's presence in the room. "She can make the MPI say anything she pleases."

"The earlier test is disturbing," Bergman said. "It may not be a good data point from which to compare. The fact that the more recent test shows a more normal personality could simply be an indication of a disturbed mental state for the first test. Drugs or fears of the treatment may have compromised it."

"I wasn't on any drugs at the time," Sarah said. "And I don't ever recall being afraid of the treatment. Eager, maybe. Not afraid."

"But you recall taking the earlier test," Czerny said. "Did you change your responses deliberately to change the assessment?"

"I have access to all of the personalities now," Sarah said. "The first time, only Cordelia took the test. I'm still integrating them all, but I tried to get a consensus view from everyone. You see, I'm interested in the results as much as you are. Perhaps more. I want to know myself, my new, complete self."

Czerny looked doubtful. "You want us to believe that the treatments were 100% successful, and that Doctor Williams has come up with a completely functional cure for Wellman's. I can see how the two of you would benefit from that, financially and professionally."

"Doctor Czerny," Sarah said, "Everyone looks at life through the window of their own experience. You will believe what you believe and I'm OK with that. My window has expanded quite a bit, and I look at life differently now than Cordelia Bellingham did eight weeks ago. She didn't watch her parents die, she never fell in love, and she never played a musical instrument, or painted a painting. Whether the treatments for Wellman's are to thank for my transformation, or whether I just needed the right set of cues, I am a whole person today."

"You realize," Morgenstern said, "That if we agree with you, and state that for the court, that you could be on trial for murder."

"I'll take my chances," Sarah said. "I've survived worse."

When the doctors had gone, Sarah went back to her room. The ad had another reply: *Coming to pick up the items. There by 11:00 am tomorrow.*

She sent some emails, and worked on some more sketches of her parents, until long after the sun had fallen into the waves, and the evening fog had obliterated the stars. She washed the charcoal from her hands, and walked out onto the glassed-in balcony. The thin crescent moon was also about to set, obscured for the most part by the mist, its weak glow illuminating the clouds.

She was asleep when Douglas Warwick quietly opened the door and slipped inside. Alice Watkins shushed the guard at the door when he began to protest, and the door closed quietly behind Douglas as his eyes adjusted to the dark. Sarah had awakened.

"Hey there," she said. "You made it." She smiled at the roses.

"Not a single speeding ticket," he said.

A Distant Beacon

"I'll bet you're beat," she said, throwing open the sheets on the side of the bed closest to him. "Come on in."

"Mind if I rinse off first?" he said. "The nurse said you had a shower in here."

"Ever the romantic. The shower's in there," she said, waving towards the bathroom.

"I'll be quick," he promised.

She waited while he showered, and smiled when he came back into the room, throwing the towel behind him in the general direction of the bathroom.

"Just how tired are you?" she asked.

"Not *that* tired," he smiled, kissing her on the lips, then on the neck, and moving down.

~

When the sun rose, they repeated the welcome, this time with both of them more rested. Afterward, they lay in the bed, with the relaxed warm heaviness that comes after particularly good sex.

"I could stay in bed all day," she said.

"I have no other plans," Douglas said.

"Unfortunately, I do," Sarah said, stroking his arm. "I have some legal problems to take care of, and a visitor from New Mexico to meet at eleven, or maybe earlier."

"I made some more calls yesterday," he said. "From the car, while passing through New Mexico. I was checking the stock price all day. They're going for it."

"I saw that," she said. "I knew I had the right man for the job."

"All you need is the right network of friends," he said. "And if they aren't all in jail, you can do magic."

"Let's concentrate on staying out of jail," she said. "Both of us."

"Everything is still legal," he said. "Like I promised."

She rose onto her elbow and kissed him again. "Then it's my turn to go to work," she said, and slid out of the bed.

He joined her in the shower, which took longer than usual. When they were dressed, she suggested breakfast in the dining hall. "You're going to love Walter," she said.

Peter Thompson called her two hours later. "That package has arrived," he said, conspiratorially.

"Tell the package hello for me, and bring him straight here," Sarah said. "The big conference room. Ask him what he'd like for lunch,

A Distant Beacon

and let him know the chef likes to show off. With an hour and a half to prepare, he can do wonders."

"Will do," Thompson grinned. She disconnected before he could hand the phone to 'the package'. She wanted to wait until she could see him in person before she broke the mystery of what he might look like today. She hadn't seen the man in seven years.

"Shall I put in my request?" Douglas asked.

"Sorry," Sarah said. "This meeting is going to have to stay very private. For his sake, not mine. You'll be on your own for lunch today."

"I can probably manage," Douglas smiled. "I have some calls to make anyway. Leak a little bit more information to the right ears."

Sarah was nervously waiting in the big conference room. Somehow, over the years Timothy Muller had become her father figure. He had taught her, coached her, and chastised her when she let him down, and his approval meant a lot to her. Would he like the person she had become?

She played with the papers in front of her, and checked the time constantly on the tablet computer. Finally, the door opened, and Peter Thompson ushered in the slender man with the receding hairline and white beard.

"Anna," he said, taking her hands in his. "It's been too long."

"I'm sorry about that," she said. "I was building a new life."

"Rather successfully," he said. "When Wilson Bellingham started making news, I was a little concerned. It seemed a little rash, but all the players were dead, and no one seemed to connect him to the company. Still, I kept track."

"You should have bought stock," Sarah said, smiling.

"I'm sure Tygaard stock is in my pension plan somewhere," he said. "Fortune 500, after all."

"There's a pension plan you don't know about," Sarah said. "A trust, in case something happened to Cordelia Bellingham. She had a will that gave Tygaard to her foundation, so I had to make special provisions for the friends she didn't know about."

"You didn't have to do that," he said.

"Yes, I did. I told you, the others really didn't know about one another. Or me. I'd surface occasionally, and I always tried to contact you. But I could tell when they were about to take over again, and I'd hide all the paints and burn any letters, and then I'd feel myself slipping away again."

"So how long do you think we have this time?" he asked.

"Forever, I think," she said. "Theresa left a note for Cordelia, and she figured it out. Got help. Built this place," she said, waving her hands at the walls. "There's a treatment. It seems to be working. All the alters are together. I have their memories, all of them."

"Building a life," he said.

"Yes, building a life. Again. But this time as a whole person."

"But with some baggage," he said. "This legal nonsense."

"Not nonsense," she said. "They know about the Mexicans. And the Wilson Bellingham part has to be handled very carefully, or the whole company may end up in the tank."

"What do they know about the Mexicans?" he asked.

A Distant Beacon

She got out the reports from the folder on the table. "They think I pulled the trigger," she said. "Did the mess on the fence. To them all crazy people are capable of anything."

"When is the next hearing?" he asked.

"Four o'clock this afternoon."

"Then we'd better get a story ready," he said. He opened his briefcase. "I came prepared."

They worked through lunch. Jameson arrived an hour after that, with the rest of the legal team. Sarah and Muller filled them in on their ideas, and together they came to an agreement on how to proceed.

~

Judge Richard Ramsay addressed the lawyers in the room, and the court reporter.

"This hearing has been sealed at the request of the United States Drug Enforcement Agency," he said. "All parties in this room have signed binding confidentiality agreements. No part of what is discussed here will become part of public record as long as all parties involved still live."

He straightened in his chair, and looked towards the prosecutor. "You may proceed," he said.

"The state calls Cordelia Bellingham to the stand," the prosecutor said.

"This is an informal hearing," Ramsay said. "You may address Mrs. Bellingham where she sits. There will be no swearing in at this time."

The prosecutor looked at the judge, a bit discomfited by the unusual proceedings. He recovered, and turned towards Sarah.

"If it please the court," he said, a little uncertainly, turning back to the judge, "Since we have Mr. Muller here, I thought I'd start with the questions relating to Santiago Garcia and Ernesto Rodriguez."

"Proceed," Ramsay said.

"Mrs. Bellingham, did you know these two people?" he asked.

"I did," she said.

"Can you describe the nature of your relationship with these men?"

"Those men boarded *The Quest* and shot my parents, and then set fire to the boat," Sarah said.

"That would seem to be motive for murder," the prosecutor said.

"Is that a question?" Sarah asked.

"Did you harbor ill-will towards these two men?" the prosecutor asked.

"Morganna Wilson certainly did," Sarah said.

"Could you tell the court who Morganna Wilson is?" he said.

"The daughter of Lee and Clarice Wilson, the people they killed," Sarah said.

"And that is you," he clarified.

"Yes," Sarah agreed.

"Did you wish them dead?" he asked.

"I did," she said.

"Did you kill these men?" he asked.

"I did," Sarah said.

This took both the prosecutor and Ramsay by surprise. Each looked at the other, and then back at Sarah.

"Your honor," Muller said, standing up. "She did so while working for the DEA. She was part of our task force on the Del Rio cartel. She arranged for certain documents to become public. Those documents caused members of the Del Rio gang to execute Garcia and Rodriguez. She knew what the outcome would be, and acted against DEA policies, but she was under my direction at the time."

"Knowingly creating a situation that leads to murder is still murder," the prosecutor said.

"That is true," Muller said. "But all of these actions took place in Nogales Mexico, and are not under the jurisdiction of this court."

"But I am sure the Mexican authorities might want to question Mrs. Bellingham about these murders," the prosecutor said.

"The Mexican authorities aided her in the release of the documents," Muller said. "They'd probably like to give her a medal."

"Your honor," the prosecutor said, "Those two killings sparked a major drug war that lasted for years, and caused hundreds of casualties."

"And broke up one of the world's most successful drug cartels," Muller said. "No cartel has ever been as effective since. Those wars took out most of the intelligence and business history of that organization. The lessons they had learned went to the grave with them."

"Your honor, she just admitted to murder," the prosecutor said.

"The DEA would like the details of this to remain secret," Muller said. "Since this court has no jurisdiction, we ask that our remaining agents in the field, and Miss Wilson, be protected by keeping this record sealed."

"Your honor," the prosecutor said, "There are two other murders."

Jameson stood up. "And what would those be?" he asked.

"Wilson Bellingham and Arthur Woods," the prosecutor said.

"Your honor," Jameson said, facing Ramsay. "I would like to present to the court Arthur Woods. Could the bailiff please escort him in?"

"Woods is alive?" Ramsay asked.

A Distant Beacon

"He's waiting outside, with the rest of our legal team," Jameson said.

"Bailiff, bring Mr. Woods in," Ramsay said.

They waited while Arthur Woods was brought into the room.

"Mr. Woods," Ramsay said, looking down from the bench. "Would you be willing to provide fingerprints to prove you are the person you say you are?"

"Sure," Woods said, smiling.

"Your honor," Jameson said. "I would like to present a notarized statement, with thumb print, made by Mr. Woods just yesterday. We also present a statement by the chief of police as to the match of that print to the records on file with the Department of Motor Vehicles, as well as prints made at that time in front of the chief himself."

"The state would like to do its own fingerprinting," the prosecutor said.

"The state will have that opportunity," Ramsay said. "In the meantime, I will see these documents," he said, accepting the papers from Jameson.

"At this time," Jameson said, "We would like to ask the prosecutor for any proof in his possession that Wilson Bellingham is an actual person, and not the corporation of that name started by Walter Bellingham and Lee Wilson, father of the woman accused of murdering that corporation."

"Of course he's a real person," the prosecutor said. "He's her husband!"

"Your honor," Jameson said. "We would like to present the court with this document, delivered to the State of Nevada, asking for the annulment of the marriage of Cordelia Watson to Wilson Bellingham, on the grounds of false identity, dated seven years ago." He handed Ramsay the document.

"Did this annulment take place?" Ramsay asked.

"The State of Nevada has apparently ignored the document," Jameson said, "as no actual person appeared in court. But the filing occurred on the date listed, and the statute of limitations for falsifying legal documents in the State of Nevada expired three years ago, four years after the court was notified by accepting this document."

The prosecutor looked at Ramsay and Jameson in astonishment.

Ramsay wasted no more time. "This court can see no case before it under which it has any jurisdiction. If the prosecution has no evidence that Wilson Bellingham is a person, that Arthur Woods is dead, or that Santiago Garcia and Ernesto Rodriguez were U.S. citizens or were killed on U.S. soil, then no further business in this matter remains for this court. Does the prosecution have this evidence?"

"No, your honor," the prosecutor said quietly.

"Then I think all involved should be thankful that these proceedings are sealed. Court is adjourned. Mrs. Bellingham, you are free to go."

~

A Distant Beacon

The party at the Bellingham estate was quickly put together, but nonetheless well attended. Hospital staff mixed with local politicians and businessmen and women, lawyers, judges, and friends. Dick Ramsay and Michael Jameson stood at the balcony railing, drinks in their hands, watching Sarah accompany the band on a large grand piano, a new addition to the large hall.

"She pulled it off," Jameson said, taking a sip of his brandy.

"I told you the annulment would come in handy," Ramsay said.

"You always were the better lawyer," Jameson said.

"Who's the guy she's with?" Ramsay asked, indicating Douglas Warwick, sitting at the piano bench with Sarah, his arm around her waist.

"Someone she met in Atlanta," Jameson said. "I did a background check. You don't want to know."

"Am I likely to see him in my court?" Ramsay asked, smiling.

"She says she can keep him out of trouble. She's making up a new position for him at Tygaard. V.P. of Fraud Prevention. Just a token, nobody reports to him, but I can assure you he's qualified."

"Oh boy," Ramsay said. "That kind of qualification."

"That's how she found you and me," Jameson said. "And Williams. She likes damaged goods."

Ramsay raised his glass. "To damaged goods," he said. The glasses touched, and were soon empty.

~

"So, I get immunity?" Alice asked, looking up at Reynolds.

"No," Reynolds said. "For that, you would need to talk to the D.A. What I'm offering is better. The D.A. will never know."

"You already have Dunbar, why do you need me?" Alice asked.

"He doesn't exactly make a good witness. He ate all the merchandise after shooting Wallace. His brain doesn't exactly work all that well anymore. They have him in Salinas Valley, and no one expects him to ever get out."

"But he gave up Marvin," she said.

"He also gave up his dog and his high school sweetheart. But Marvin we had paper on," Reynolds said.

"So you need me to give you Marvin."

"And in return, we mention nothing about why you were there when Wallace went down," Reynolds said.

"And I just trust you," Alice said.

"I don't see you having a lot of choice," Reynolds said. "A nurse arrested for possession for sale has a hard time finding a new job in her profession."

"You don't have anything on me, other than what Petey Dunbar said. Are you going to arrest his dog, too?"

"I'm asking nice," Reynolds said. "I need this one."

"Yeah, I heard about how your last bust ended up," Alice said.

"But this time we have a body. And from here on out, if there's no body, I don't want to hear about it. But we were talking about *you*.

We can just keep watching you, you know. We'll catch you eventually."

"Except I don't do that anymore," Alice said.

"Once an addict," Reynolds said.

"My mom gave up smoking," Alice said. "That stuff Petey ate isn't even addictive."

"What was it, anyway?" Reynolds asked.

"An experimental drug," Alice said. "Nice buzz if you snort it, but it is designed to overload the part of you that dreams if you get it in small doses. Shuts down the dreaming. They give it to Walter in the morning, and by nighttime it's worn off, so he only dreams at night."

"Walter," Reynolds said. "You mean the doctor?"

"Walter is a podiatrist. Or he was before his accident. Now he can't tell what is real. He sees a soap opera and thinks it's happening in real life. Thinks people are plotting, scheming, killing people, and sleeping around, all that stuff that happens in the soaps."

"Like talking in their sleep about killing their husband," Reynolds said, realization dawning.

"That was from the Doctor Hathaway show," Alice said. "We watch it together in the mornings."

Reynolds wanted to change the subject. "So, all I need is for you to arrange a buy from Marvin. We get him for the drugs, and we have probable cause to search his place. We find the bullets he put in the gun he gave to Dunbar, and we connect him to Jack Wallace's murder."

"The bullets are all you need?" Alice asked.

"All gunpowder has micro flakes in it, ever since the Ryan Act. All those little flakes tell us which batch the ammo came from. We have Dunbar's gun. We find the bullets at Marvin Bailiss' place, and we have the link."

"But I'm not around when all this goes down," Alice said. "All I do is vouch for the buyer."

Reynolds was not pleased. "We can work it that way, if you think he'll go for it. I had you in mind as the buyer."

"He knows I don't do street stuff. That wouldn't work," Alice said. "But I can say one of my patients is being released, and needs some retail therapy."

"He'd go for that?"

"He has in the past," Alice said. "Of course then it was true. The guy was in real pain, just couldn't pay his hospital bill."

"You're a regular Florence Nightingale," Reynolds.

Alice ignored the sarcasm. "So you forget you ever met me, if I do this."

"Nothing goes on paper," Reynolds said.

"I'll need a description of the buyer, and a name," she said.

"His name is David Archer," Reynolds said. "Alcoholic, about five ten, brown hair, one sixty or so."

"Have him come with his arm in a sling," Alice said. "If you need a sling, drop by the hospital and I'll get you one."

"So we have a deal," Reynolds said.

"Like I have a choice. Yeah, we have a deal."

~

Walter looked into the doctor's eyes and considered what he was going to say. "You think this will actually work," he stated, not asking a question.

"The process is transferable," Williams said. "We can retrain your brain, like we did for Arthur and Cordelia."

"But they didn't have the same..." Walter said, hesitating. "Condition."

"No, you're right. But the same approach should apply. We increase the plasticity, and retrain. It's like getting to be a child again. Children can learn languages so easily, where adults struggle for a lifetime."

"But Arthur forgot who he was," Walter said.

"Not permanently," Williams said. "He's fine now."

"But I'd lose George," Walter said.

Williams was quiet, considering Walter's face.

"George isn't real," Williams said quietly.

"I know," Walter said. "But he's my best friend."

"You have other friends," Williams said. "You have Cordelia. She's paying for your treatments, and she'll be paying for this. That's quite a friend. And once you are competent, you'll make more friends."

"Once I'm normal, you mean."

"Well, yes, but that's such a value-laden word," Williams said.

"Unlike competent," Walter said sadly.

"Are you happy here? Williams asked.

A Distant Beacon

"Happy?" Walter asked. "I have moments. But no, I haven't been happy in a long time."

"Wouldn't you like to fix that?"

"At what cost?" Walter asked. "I've had the happy pills. What good is happiness when your life is just... empty?"

"This would be different," Williams said. "You'd be able to live in the real world. Meet people. Have a job, maybe a family. You'd be..."

"Normal," Walter finished for him. "Without the dreams."

"Normal people have dreams," Williams said quietly.

"I remember," Walter said. "I was normal once."

Williams looked at his watch. "No one is going to force you into a decision. Take all the time you like. I'll be around if you have any more questions, and you can decide any time you like, and change your mind as many times as you need. It is a big deal. Life-changing, in every sense."

He stood up, and straightened his lab coat. Walter watched him leave.

"You know you have to do it," George said.

"I know," Walter replied.

"You've always known I'm not real," George said. "I'm in your head. You made me up. Everything I know, you already know."

"I know," Walter said, smiling at the repetition.

"So why give the doctor such a hard time?"

"I'm not ready," Walter said. "I'm scared."

"You'll still be scared when you're ready," George said.

"It's not just that," Walter said. "All my friends are here."

"Cordelia won't be."

"But Alice will, and Doctor Williams, and even Artie is staying on in the kitchen," Walter said.

"So come and visit," George said. "Or volunteer. Heck, maybe the hospital needs a podiatrist. I'll bet Cordelia could make that happen, even if they didn't. She owns the place."

"I can't ask her to do that," Walter said.

"Then don't. Try it on your own. Ask Williams to check it out for you. But you know you can't stay like this when there's a cure. And Cordelia would rather pay for a podiatrist than a patient, anyway."

"You do always give good advice," Walter said.

"Of course," said George. "I'm the smartest one in the room."

~

A Distant Beacon

Douglas Warwick put down the journal, still open to the last page of the timeline, and looked up. All he said was a quiet "Wow."

Sarah waited, but when nothing more substantial came, she said, "So now you know who you're sleeping with. Still want to hang around the murderess?"

He looked down at the journal in his lap. "They killed your parents," he said. He could tell from her face that it was the wrong thing to say.

"So that made it my turn?" she said. "Tag, you're the murderer. I could never do that again. There were women and children at those funerals. Is it their turn now? I hid behind Cordelia for seven years, hiding from the fact that I did something that no one could undo. Started a war that killed hundreds of people. How many killers did I create? How many widows? How many lonely children with those pictures in their heads forever?"

"I never thought of it from that point of view," he said.

"It's an abstract thing until you actually kill someone," she said. "It was for me. Justice. Fear. Hate. I didn't hate their children. I just took their daddies away. Forever. Do you think those kids knew what their fathers had done? What did I turn them into? Is that how all this started in the first place?"

"You've thought a lot about this," he said.

"I have to. I have to know who I am. It's time to stop hiding."

"So who are you?" he asked. "What should I call you now?"

She laughed. "Call me Anna," she said. "Everyone who really loved me called me Anna."

www.ingramcontent.com/pod-product-compliance
Lightning Source LLC
Chambersburg PA
CBHW032045240626
47154CB00003B/1087